Albatross Bay

Roger Harvey

Albatross Bay

Irrepressible young adventurers Lucy and Sam travel from London in Dad's motorcycle-and-sidecar for the holiday of a lifetime on the wild Northumbrian coast. In their newly-discovered world of beach, rocks, and an uninhabited island, a tale of romance and excitement unfolds to storms and sunshine and the mysterious music of the sea--but they soon have to deal with grown-up passions as well as the wind and weather. Roger Harvey's enchanting tale of the mermaid and the millionaire, the poet with the boat, and the one-parent family with the motorbike offers a witty and magical feast for all ages.

Dedicated to
the real
Lucy and Sam
and
everyone who wants the best holiday ever.

Chapter 1   The Ride to the North

It took two days to reach the bay, travelling from London in the two-seater sidecar of Dad's motorcycle. As the heavy machine growled steadily up the Great North Road, Lucy realised there were two of almost everything on this trip: two seats in the sidecar, two wheels on the motorcycle, two exhaust pipes roaring away just behind her head, two children in the sidecar--but only one of Dad.

It would have been good, thought Lucy, if there had been a Mum as well: not simply to make two parents in a neat way, but to complete the family and make Dad properly happy again. Of course there had been a Mum, but she had died shortly after Lucy's brother Sam had been born, and Lucy could never be sure whether the Mum she faintly remembered was the real Mum or only the Mum of the photographs and Dad's stories. It was sad that she had died, but they were not a sad family. In fact they made a very happy family, Lucy realised once again, and Dad was a wonderful Dad.

There he was in his thick leather jacket and boots, sitting beside and above Lucy and Sam, steering the big bike with his leather-gloved hands, avoiding bumps and holes in the road, watching out for dangerous drivers, looking down every few minutes at the children to check they were safe. There was only one of Dad--and it was great fun to be going on holiday with him.

Last night they had slept in an elegant hotel at Doncaster which Dad said had cost almost as much as their hire of the tiny wooden cottage they would reach tonight--but he said they could afford it because the rest of the holiday would cost so little. So the motorcycle and sidecar had rested overnight beside big cars in a fascinating, raftered garage, once a stable when the hotel had been a coaching inn. Tonight the machine would be under its canvas cover outside their cottage in the sand dunes. Tonight they would sleep beside the sea!

"Not far now," Dad shouted. "We're into Northumberland--and look, there's the sea."

Lucy and Sam craned their necks to find the Eastern horizon--and there, far beyond the quiet fields of the coastal plain, they could glimpse a straight strip of sea the colour of a fisherman's jersey. It still looked a long way away, but they knew the curve of the coast was sweeping in to run closer to the Great North Road and that soon they would turn due East to head straight for that dark, flat line. It looked magical, mysterious, and inviting under a Summer evening sky now clearing to a vast and open ice-blue dome, with the very first stars appearing.

"D'you see them?" asked Sam. "They're millions and billions and trillions of miles away but they look as if you could reach up and touch them."

"You'd need very long arms," replied Lucy. "Is it much further, Dad?"

"I reckon about twenty miles from here."

"I love travelling in the sidecar when it's just getting dark like this," said Sam. "It's like flying through the Universe."

"We're doing that anyway," Lucy reminded him, "just by being on our own planet."

"I like this more, though: just going that bit faster--and I love the bike noise, don't you? It gets right into you. You don't get that feeling just standing on the Earth, you've got to travel in Dad's sidecar."

"Don't know," answered Lucy. "The Earth might make a noise as it moves--only no-one's heard it out there in Space."

Dad throttled back slightly.

"Centuries ago," he explained, "people did think all the planets and stars made a sound as they moved around one another. They called it the Music of the Spheres."

"Wow! I'd love to hear that."

Lucy put her arms around Sam's shoulders just a little lower than hers in the front seat of the sidecar. "Maybe, when we're very happy like this, we *are* hearing it."

And at that idea, Sam fell silent--but the motorcycle growled on as Dad opened the throttle again and they sped down empty country roads, the sea straight ahead of them and the stars above.

Chapter 2   The House above the Beach

It was the Skylarks that woke them: a constant stream of sweet birdsong seeming to rise straight above the thin roof, soar up and up into a magnificent sky of blue and golden light, then cascade down again over the whole house, through its square windows, and into their little wooden-walled bedroom. How many Skylarks were up there? How high were they climbing? Would it be possible to find them against the dazzling blue?

"Let's get up and see!"

Sam was first out of his narrow bed, Lucy following from her bed on the opposite side of the room. They burst out through the front door--and there was the vast seascape right before their eyes: a long, wide, yellow-sanded beach curving gently from a village and its harbour at the Northern end, past a little island, beneath their door here in the dunes, and all the way South to a ruined castle on its great black cliff. The light was dazzling, the beach was empty, the sea was flat calm and quiet. Only the Skylarks rinsed the sparklng air with their delightful song of open dunes, fresh grass, pure air, salty smells, blue sea, the tiny wooden house, hot sand under bare feet, the open country with its distant hills behind and the luminous water below, the one small island, and the vast sea beyond it.

"Norway is straight out there," said Lucy, pointing over the North Sea.

"And two Skylarks are straight up there," said Sam, pointing higher than the early morning sun.

"Yes, I see them."

"And I see you."

It was Dad, suddenly standing in the doorway behind them.

"We wondered if you'd be awake," said Lucy. "It's not even six o'clock."

"I know, but I'm completely awake. I thought you two would be up early, so I've made us breakfast."

"Hooray for breakfast!" cried Sam. "Our first breakfast in the tiny house on the forgotten seashore."

"We're going to be marooned sailors," explained Lucy.

"We're going to fight off pirate attacks," added Sam. "We're going to be explorers. We're going to look for treasure. We're going to be zoologists and ornithologists and map-makers."

"We're going to do all sorts of things," grinned Dad, "after breakfast. Come on."

Back inside the kitchen, which was also the main room of the house with the best views over the sea, Dad had been filling cereal bowls and making toast.

"No eggs this morning, I'm sorry to say, but we'll get some from the farm tomorrow."

"How d'you know there are eggs at the farm?" asked Sam. "How d'you know there *is* a farm?"

"I told you," explained Dad, "I've been here before. I drove around here years ago and stayed overnight, but not in this cottage. I stayed in the village, and I thought what a wonderful place it would be to bring Lucy and Sam one Summer."

"And this is the Summer?"

"It certainly is," smiled Dad.

"It's going to be our best holiday ever," said Lucy.

* * *

The night before, everyone had been too tired to do anything but roll out their sleeping bags on the wooden beds; Dad in one bedroom, Lucy and Sam in the other. They had left their cases and bags mostly unpacked in the main room, washed quickly in the small bathroom, brushed their teeth, and dropped into bed. But this morning they all felt very different: no-one was tired, everyone was eager to set up their holiday home and begin discovering the secrets of the beach, dunes, rocks, and pools so temptingly spread out under their doorstep.

"A proper base-camp first," stated Sam. "Every explorer knows that. Check for snakes, poisonous spiders, soldier ants, and bloodstains of the last explorers massacred by cannibals."

"Not very likely," said Lucy. "You can check for germs, though," she added, handing him a bottle of disinfectant.

They cleaned the tiny wash-basin, bath, and toilet, and set out their towels, face-cloths, soaps, and toothbrushes. Then they unpacked the rest of their kit and stowed it neatly in the various rooms. Dad was an expert at packing things into bags and cases to go on and around the motorcycle and sidecar, and he had ensured they had brought everything they might need for a Summer holiday at the coast: swimming-trunks and bathing-costumes, beach shoes and walking boots, haversacks, wellingtons, jeans, shirts, belts, woolly jumpers and waterproof jackets, sunhats, and shorts. Lucy had packed one 'smart' dress and one pair of 'good' brown shoes, but she expected to spend most of the time in shirts and shorts with gym-shoes or no shoes. Sam had packed his book of British birds, but since he was now going to be an explorer, he expected to make more use of his compass and Dad's binoculars. Then there were cooking utensils and the portable paraffin stove.

"Not that we're likely to need it," said Dad. "Look at this." He examined an old iron stove in a corner of the kitchen with its tall black pipe running straight up through the roof. "Like something from a Prisoner-of-War camp."

"You were never a P.O.W., were you, Dad?"

"No," he grinned, "they never got me. By the way, if you're thinking of escaping, don't start your tunnel from under the stove: it's always the first place the guards look."

They carried on stowing their food and equipment: cups and plates, knives forks and spoons, vacuum flasks for picnics, tins of dried milk and packets of biscuits, jars of jam and marmalade, baked beans.....

".....and the tin-opener," said Lucy. "I'm putting it in this drawer. See where it is now, everybody, and don't forget."

Then there were the beds to arrange properly. It was probably going to be too warm to sleep inside the sleeping-bags, so they were shaken and rolled out once more as mattresses with a light sheet over each one. With pillows nicely plumped up in freshly-laundered pillowcases, hats and bags hanging on the bed-ends and shoes placed neatly underneath, the bedrooms looked cosy and inviting even in the middle of the morning when nobody wanted to go to sleep.

"There," declared Lucy. "Nobody would *want* to escape from here now."

"All the same," replied Sam, making himself sound dramatically weary, "I wouldn't mind a holiday from all the housework."

"It's starting now," smiled Dad. "I must go over to the farm to arrange our supplies of eggs and milk. It's about half a mile away across the fields behind the dunes. We might even be able to buy our bread there if the farmer's wife bakes it. You've never had fresh farmhouse bread, have you?"

"Not yet, Dad."

"You'll like it, I promise."

"So while you're shopping," asked Lucy, "can we go exploring?"

"That's the idea," said Dad. "Don't get lost now," he added. "I'll only be an hour or so, but best not to stray out of sight of the house until you know your way around here."

"We won't get lost," grinned Sam. "I'm going to start making our map, and I'll need to keep the house in sight as my key point."

"Good stuff," said Dad, checking the money in his wallet. "No swimming, mind you, not until I'm with you. I believe there are very strong currents along this coast."

"We won't even get wet," promised Sam.

"I wouldn't like to bet on that," smiled Dad. "See you later."

"Come on, Sam!" shouted Lucy, jumping out through the door. "I'll race you to the water's edge."

"That's unfair! It's all downhill in soft sand and I'm weighed down with my map-making equipment and your legs are longer!"

Chapter 3   Explorers

Down at the water's edge the bay looked a different place. The sand was pale and hard with no seaweed to spoil its perfect smoothness and very few seashells. Down here, the empty beach and the flat sea seemed vast and Lucy and Sam felt small. The morning was still and warm under a cloudless sky. The only sound was a soft rippling as tiny wavelets came gently up the beach--but there was nothing gentle about the shocking coldness of the water as it lapped around the children's ankles.

"We said we wouldn't get wet," Sam reminded Lucy, sounding pleased to be back on warm sand.

"Wet feet don't count on a beach holiday, silly." Lucy was looking back at the house. "Doesn't it look small from here?"

"It is small, but I love it already. Don't you?"

"Of course I do. Oh--look at that." She indicated a heavy-bodied bird, white and grey like a seagull, but hardly moving its wings at all as it glided low across the water. "It's a little Albatross."

"That's not an Albatross," Sam corrected her, "that's a Fulmar."

"I know it's a Fulmar," replied Lucy, "but Fulmars are distantly related to Albatrosses--that's in your bird book--and they glide in almost the same way. Let's call this place Albatross Bay on your map."

"I like that," declared Sam, following the bird's flight Southwards towards the ruined castle on its black cliff. "Even if it's not a real Albatross, it's a great name: Albatross Bay."

"Perhaps we'll see a real Albatross one day," said Lucy wistfully.

"Too far North," said Sam flatly. "Talking of North," he continued in a businesslike way, "let's climb that big dune just before the river flows out across the beach there. We'll make it a lookout hill and use my compass to find North, then we can start our map."

"Come on then."

They went down the beach, paddled in the warmer water of the shallow river as it emptied itself into the sand, and climbed the lookout dune. Soon they were struggling up on all fours as the sand turned powder soft and the hill became steeper. Their efforts were well rewarded at the top. They enjoyed a wonderful sense of being up in the sky, and the air itself seemed to run and shimmer like water. Even on this still day in the middle of Summer it seemed Winter-fresh and Nordic-pure. They breathed it in and drew new vigour from it--and the

15

view from the top was even better than from their cottage. They saw at once that there was another lookout dune almost as high just across the river.

"We'll call this one the North Lookout Dune and that one the South Lookout Dune," decided Sam, making a rough sketch in his notebook of what could be seen from this vantage point.

"Yes," said Lucy, "and that can be Shelduck River." She pointed to a large multicoloured duck paddling across the widest part of the stream where it had become almost a lake. "The first Shelduck I've ever seen. It's bigger than I thought, and prettier. The colours are wonderful. There could be a pair."

"They might nest there," said Sam.

"Probably. I wonder what Shelducklings look like."

"Shelduck River." Sam marked it on his sketch. "I'm drawing that island over there but we need to go and explore it properly."

"It's not strictly an island now the tide is out," observed Lucy.

Low tide had revealed a rocky causeway across the sand, a stone-strewn path to the rugged outcrop with the tiny patch of grass which made it a true island when the water was high. From the first moment they had seen it, the island had been the most fascinating feature of the bay: more dramatic than the castle, more fun than the beach, more interesting than the village, more attractive than anything. It was sitting there in the way that islands do, inviting adventurers, just waiting to be explored.

"It was an island last night," insisted Sam.

"So--all it means is that we mustn't get caught by the tide....."

"Of course we won't," interrupted Sam. "It'll be hours yet before it comes in, and Dad will be back soon anyway."

".....but on this first expedition it was a great idea to keep the best 'til last," grinned Lucy. "What could be better than exploring an island? We'll claim it for our very own."

"How?" asked Sam. "Shall we plant a flag?"

"Better than that. We'll build a cairn of stones that'll last for ever."

"And bury something under it?"

"Yes, if you like."

"What?"

"We'll think of something."

Chapter 4   The Mermaid

From the beginning of its rocky causeway, the island looked much bigger than it had seemed from the house or the lookout dune. The causeway was longer than it had looked, and Lucy and Sam found it was hard going over seaweed-covered stones to reach the flatter rocks and huge boulders of the island itself. After a strenuous scramble-- sometimes easier on all fours than risking a fall or a twisted ankle--they stood at last on the miniature central plain. Long grass sprouted between the rocks and bunches of sea-pinks bloomed under the sun.

"It's like a tiny garden," said Lucy.

"Yes," answered Sam, "a garden in the middle of the sea, the last garden in England before you get to Norway."

"Or the first, if you're coming the other way."

"Anyway, we've found it," asserted Sam. "It's our holiday island garden for ever now."

There appeared to be no animals or birds on the island, and certainly no people. The only sign of life was a flight of Oystercatchers sweeping around them, as smart as a squadron of military aircraft in their black, white, and red markings, and heading back to feed on the shore.

"Uninhabited," confirmed Lucy.

"I'm pleased, aren't you?"

"Yes, of course. We'll come back and build our cairn when there's more time. Let's look at the far coast before we go. I think there'll be a little cliff on the seaward side."

"We might see more Fulmars."

"There could even be seals."

It was only a few paces to the Eastern edge of the island, then Lucy and Sam had to scramble on all fours again to make their way up a steep slope of rock. Just as Lucy had guessed, it did end in a small cliff falling straight into the sea; but, when they peeped over the edge and looked down on to a short coastline of gently sea-swilled rocks, they didn't see Fulmars or seals--they saw a woman.

She was sitting on a rock, staring lazily out to sea. She looked as if she had just come out of the water after a swim and was drying herself in the warm sunshine. Her legs were curled underneath her and one hand was resting on the rock. She was running the fingers of her other hand through her short yellow hair.

The children had drawn back in surprise and looked at each other. Now they edged their heads over the cliff once more. The woman was still there and still hadn't seen them. There was something exciting, mysterious, and sad about her--all at the same time. Who was she? Where had she come from? What was she going to do? Why was she sitting on her lonely rock, looking out to sea? How had she discovered the quietest, most isolated, most secretive place in the whole bay and claimed it as her own by sitting there so languidly, so confidently, so beautifully?

"She's a mermaid," whispered Lucy.

"Mermaids don't have legs," objected Sam.

"They do when they come out of the sea. On land, they have legs. All the old stories say so."

"But she can't be a *real* mermaid," continued Sam quietly, "not like in the stories. Real mermaids have long hair--very long hair. They use it to cover their bare bosoms. She's got hers covered by a swimsuit."

"I've never seen a swimsuit like hers." Lucy sounded very impressed. "Look at it: bright purple, and no straps on the shoulders. I wish my swimsuit was as modern as hers. She could be a French fashion model."

"A long way from France," whispered Sam.

"I wonder where she's left her bags and things and the rest of her clothes."

"Well, if you say she's a mermaid," argued Sam, "she won't have any bags and things, and she won't wear clothes."

"But a modern mermaid would wear *some* clothes *sometimes*--like that swimsuit."

"Oh!" Sam interrupted. "She's moving her head!"

They dodged back down behind the cliff's edge.

"Why are we hiding from her?" whispered Lucy with a giggle.

"I don't know. Why *are* we?"

"I don't know. Are you afraid of her, Sam?"

"No. Why should I be afraid of her?

"Because she's a beautiful woman."

"I'm not old enough to be afraid of beautiful women. Anyway, how d'you know she's beautiful?"

"I saw her face.....and her figure in that swimsuit. She's beautiful. And you're right: grown-up men *would* be afraid of her."

"Well I've already said I'm not afraid of her. Are you?"

"No."

"Then why don't we say hello to her?"

"I don't know!"

They stifled their giggles and stared at each other: a stare that said 'one more look over the edge'.....but before they could move, a loud 'sploosh' echoed around the rocks. The children's heads popped up.

"Wow!" Sam's exclamation was matched by Lucy's wide-eyed stare. "She really could be a mermaid. That was a brilliant dive. Look, she's still under the water!"

At last the woman's head did break the surface after her long underwater glide out to sea. Lucy and Sam dodged back down behind the rock.

"She's amazing," said Lucy.

"She's weird," said Sam.

"We mustn't let her see we've been watching her," cautioned Lucy.

"Why not?"

"I don't know--but let's not."

"Okay."

"And let's get back to the house. Dad will be expecting us."

They stood up to go--but they didn't get very far.

"Hello there!" It was a voice from the sea. "You on the island!"

They felt that sudden terror of being 'found out'; shocked and guilty and in some kind of nameless trouble--and they knew it was the mermaid's voice. There was a moment when they thought they might just run straight back to the beach, but of course they didn't. They had to turn and face her--and when they did they saw she had swum back to the island and was standing up in the sea, the shallow water round her knees. Once more she was running her fingers through her short hair, shaking water from her ears, her upturned face catching the sunlight. As Lucy had seen, it was a beautiful face, but it wasn't smiling.

"Do you know it's very dangerous to play on that island?" Her voice was surprisingly loud and clear as she spoke up to them like a displeased teacher. "The tide can come in quickly and you can be cut off."

Lucy found her voice.

"Yes, we know that, thank you. We were just going."

This was not going to be the end of the interview.

"Can you both swim?"

'Not as well as you,' thought Sam, but didn't say it.

"Yes," answered Lucy.

"Well that's something, but even good swimmers can be swept away here." By this time the mermaid had walked out of the sea and was back on her rock, standing with hands on the hips of her wet swimsuit, water dripping down her legs, her toes grippng the black stone. "The tides can be very dangerous." She didn't look like a mermaid to the children any more; she looked like a real woman telling them off--but while she might be a real woman, she was scarcely an ordinary one. She wasn't bothering to dry herself with her hands, just standing in the sun. The children began to see she was very beautiful indeed: from her bright golden hair cut surprisingly short and her gleaming teeth unusually white to her long strong legs and suntanned feet. "So," she continued, unimpressed by any admiring glances that might have been coming from Lucy and Sam, "are you going home now?"

"We were just going." Sam thought his own voice sounded odd, speaking to a strange lady who had just come out of the sea in a dramatic-looking purple swimsuit. He decided to say nothing more.

"We're on holiday," explained Lucy, losing her shyness. "In one of the cottages in the dunes, the one you can see, up there."

"I know it," said the woman without looking.

"We're here with our Dad."

"He should look after you better."

"He *does* look after us," answered Lucy with some annoyance. Who was this woman to tell their Dad to look after them? At the same time, Lucy felt she couldn't be too annoyed: the woman was beginning to smile at them. Then she suddenly flipped backwards off the rock and disappeared into deep water--leaving Lucy and Sam speechless, just looking at each other.

"She was angry with us," said Lucy at last. "She didn't like being discovered."

"But *we* didn't have to mind being discovered by *her*," commented Sam.

"Exactly. She was rather rude."

"But she was rather wonderful, too."

They crept back to the grassy middle of the island, scrambled over the causeway, and eventually regained the beach: breathless, as if they had been chased; awed into an unusual silence, as if they had seen something they should not have seen.

Dad's smile brightened them up.

"Hello, you two. Back safely from the first expedition, I see. How's the map coming along?"

"We've started it," answered Lucy. "We went right down to the river, saw a Shelduck, then went over to the little island. It's a wonderful island. We saw a beautiful lady sitting on a rock."

"Lucy thought she was a mermaid."

"You thought so too, secretly you did."

"No I didn't. She's a great swimmer, though. She dived in off her rock and swam out to sea underwater, must have been half a mile."

"It wasn't that far, silly. But she is beautiful."

"She's probaly a bit mad as well."

"Really?" said Dad. "Well, you've discovered all kinds of things, haven't you? Did you speak to this mad and beautiful lady swimmer?"

"No," answered Lucy. "Sam was being shy."

"You were being shy, too--at first anyway."

"I got the idea she wanted to be all alone," began Lucy. "I wasn't going to speak to her--but then she spoke to us."

"She told us off."

The children explained what had happened

"Angry and rude, eh?" Dad smiled faintly. "Perhaps she just likes being on her own. It's sometimes good to be on your own, especially in a place like this." It seemed there was nothing else to say about the mermaid. "So--what's next? I've fixed us up with milk and eggs and bread from the farm, and the farmer's wife told me a mobile shop comes to the village once a week, so we can buy the other things we need that way. Shall we walk down to the castle this afternoon?"

"Good idea," said Sam. "that end of the map isn't drawn yet."

"And we can imagine kings and queens and crusaders and knights and prisoners in the dungeons and a whole Scots army coming out of the mist."

"Easy on the mist, Lucy," smiled Dad. "We just want this good weather to keep going."

Chapter 5   A Poet with a Boat

After lunch, Dad, Lucy and Sam enjoyed a walk down the sand towards
the castle, paddling along the sea's edge as they went. The tide had
come in and the water was a little warmer in shallow places, but still icy
cold where shelving sand made it deeper. Then they had to put on their
shoes to negotiate a section of rock at the Southern end of the beach.

"Look at those amazing rocks." Dad pointed out the dark grey
boulders. "Some of them are almost perfectly round."

"And look where they're wet," added Lucy, "where they've
rolled into the water there. They look just like seals' heads."

"Seal-Head Rocks then," decided Sam, marking the feature on
his map before joining Dad and Lucy to clamber up through the dunes
and find a grassy path leading to the castle.

It made a dramatic ruin on the Southern skyline, but close up it
was less interesting than they had imagined. It was very big, built of
massive stones, and even on a still, warm day like this one it held a
sense of wind whistling over broken battlements, around collapsed
towers, and through empty windows and arrow slits. It had fallen down
to become little more than a collection of walls, and Sam was
disappointed to find there were no complete rooms or dungeons to
explore.

"The best thing is the view," admitted Lucy, feeling no
particular sense of history. "You see the whole bay from here: it's
beautiful."

"And this is where the Fulmars live," added Sam, peering down
from the battlements. "Look."

He pointed along the great dark cliff on which the castle stood.
Many gulls were flying back and forwards. The Fulmars, as usual, were
scarcely flapping their wings, while the Kittiwakes, showing their
delicate grey backs and black wing-tips, were unable to glide so well
for so long. More flapping still was being done by a number of Rock
Doves, whose nests could be seen on shelves and in crevices of the tall
cliff-face. The mewing of the gulls came wild and lonely from chill
shadows high above the faintly swishing sea.

"It will be much noisier in the breeding season," said Dad.
"We've missed it by a few months but you can still see plenty of young
birds."

They all agreed this end of the bay might have the drama of huge cliffs and black boulders and an historic castle, but the Northern end had all the charm with its uninterrupted sand, its village, boats, cottages, and of course the island. They were happy to turn back for the beach--but in doing so, Dad almost fell over the seated figure of a man whose dark jeans and jersey blended dangerously with the weathered stones of the castle wall.

"Sorry," said Dad. "We nearly didn't see you."

"That's perfectly all right." The man clambered to his feet. He was short and rather fat, older than Dad, with unkempt hair and a cultured voice. "Good afternoon."

"You meet some funny people round here," Sam whispered into Lucy's ear. "He's the second one."

"I think I prefer the first one," she whispered back.

"I beg your pardon?" Dad flashed her a severe look.

"Er.....I was saying.....it's our first time here."

"My children." Dad presented them to the stranger.

"Good afternoon," they said politely.

"I'm sorry I turned myself into a camouflaged hazard." The man was shaking their hands. "Climbing about old ruins is dangerous enough without falling over another delapidated antiquity like myself."

"What does 'delapidated' mean?" Sam whispered to Lucy.

"So old or neglected that the stones have fallen off," explained Lucy quietly.

"That's me," chuckled the stranger, who obviously thought what he had overheard was funny rather than impolite. He turned to Dad. "Are you on holiday?"

"Yes. We've come up from London."

"A long way, but worth it."

"It certainly is. The whole bay is wonderful. D'you know the history of the castle?"

Lucy and Sam guessed this was going to be one of Dad's long conversations with strangers they sometimes had to suffer. They could judge a person at once and find out everything they wanted to know in a few words, but Dad could take ages over the same business and get into all kinds of boring talk with people they'd never met before and didn't particularly want to meet again. This one was full of chatter.

".....and I do a lot of thinking here," he was saying.

"Thinking?" Dad asked if he was a scholar.

"I've been called worse. I'm a writer. History, architecture, poetry--and poetry is my favourite."

"Well, it's not every day you meet a poet," said Dad.

"Count yourself lucky," came the jovial reply. "But since you tell me these two youngsters are interested in birds, they'll have to visit the lake just behind my house."

"You live here?" asked Sam.

"Yes, for a while every Summer, in one of the cottages in the dunes."

"Then we're neighbours!" exclaimed Sam, showing their own cottage on his map. "We've called ours Skylark House, but that's not its real name. As far as I know it hasn't got a real name, but Skylark House is good because the Skylarks rise straight up above it. We hear them all the time."

"What are you going to call my house, then?" The poet asked to see Sam's map and indicated where he should mark another cottage.

"Poet's House, of course," replied Sam, writing the name on the map at once.

"Good," said the poet.

"Will you write poems about us?" asked Sam.

"You never know." He gave them a searching look. "Poets can take inspiration from anyone."

"What rhymes with Sam and Lucy?" Dad wondered, looking out to sea.

"'Jam' and 'juicy' of course," said Sam.

"I get enough of that at school," Lucy stared fiercely at Sam. "Anyway," she continued defiantly, "not all poems have to rhyme these days."

"Quite right," said the poet.

"You mustn't bother Mister Baxter with work," Dad told the children. "He's on holiday."

"Writers are never completly on holiday," smiled the poet. "Now, this bird-watching expedition. Come up to the house sometime and I can show you the lake. There's a good ornithologists' hide there. If you'd rather get closer to the real sea birds, I could take you out in my boat. It's only supposed to take three people but if it's calm we'll be quite safe with four aboard."

"You have a boat?" Sam was wide-eyed with admiration.

"Of course he has," whispered Lucy. "He's just said so."

"That's very kind of you," said Dad. "We mustn't impose upon you or take up your time."

"Nonsense. It'll be a pleasure."

They said their goodbyes and walked back up the beach.

"Well, there's something," Dad put on a big smile, "a poet with a boat."

Lucy and Sam let out a big groan.

* * *

That evening, after supper, Dad, Lucy and Sam sat on canvas chairs outside the front door of Skylark House, looking across the beach and over the sea. It was still flat and calm after a day of hot sunshine. Only lengthening shadows and a chillier blue in the sky hinted at a cooler night to come.

"Amazing weather," said Dad.

"It's going to stay light very late," observed Lucy, "like in the Land of the Midnight Sun."

"We're not *that* far North," Sam reminded her.

"And what have the adventurers planned for tomorrow's entertainment?" asked Dad.

"We could explore this lake and go bird-watching," suggested Lucy.

"Or," ventured Sam, "have a ride with the poet.....in his boat."

"Don't you start," said Lucy.

"We mustn't push ourselves on him," said Dad.

"No, but he did seem very friendly, as if he wanted some company."

"Okay, we'll call at his cottage some time tomorrow if the weather's still good."

"Last race to the water's edge and back," announced Lucy.

"I'll roll down the slope," answered Sam. "It'll be easier."

"Don't bring *all* the sand back into the house," said Dad wearily, pouring himself another glass of orange juice.

* * *

Their first night had been so disordered and everyone had been so tired that going to bed hadn't been fun--it had just been a desperate need. This night felt very different. They had made Skylark House their holiday home, everything was in place, the sleeping arrangements were clean and comfortable--and outside, under Summer stars, stretched the bay with its vast beach, fascinating dunes and rocks, the island, the village, the castle, and everything else they had seen and experienced. These things and many others began to merge and jumble in Sam's mind and he turned sideways in his bed to look across the small room to Lucy.

"What d'you think we'll dream about?" he asked.

"Motorbikes and mermaids," whispered Lucy.

"Poets and boats," suggested Sam.

"Seagulls and sleeping-bags."

"Castles and camping-stoves."

"Porridge and pirates."

"We haven't seen any porridge or pirates," objected Sam.

"Dad always packs porridge when we go away and we can pretend there are pirates."

"We don't need to pretend things here; there's so much really here."

"Shelducks and seaweed."

"Fulmars and .....we've run out of things that start with the same letter."

"We need the poet."

"We'll go in his boat tomorrow if the good weather holds."

"I'm sure it will. That'll please Dad, too."

"We mustn't wake Dad by talking too late. He'll hear us through the wall."

"Goodnight then."

"Goodnight."

And it was a good night. Lucy and Sam dreamed of all those things and many others--but since they were so tired they couldn't remember waking up and recalling the dreams. Instead, they felt a sense of peace and excitement at the same time: a secure but thrilling knowledge that in the morning they would enjoy the adventures they had planned--and find unexpected ones.

Chapter 6   A Ride on an Albatross

The next morning was bright and golden, and felt just as hot as the previous day had been, but a new Westerly breeze rippled the sea into noticeable waves and frothed up their dazzling whiteness as they beat upon the smooth sand. Lucy and Sam stepped outside into a wide, blue, sunlit world. They felt small under the big open sky, but adventurous with their happy little house behind them and the vast beach below--and once again the Skylarks trilled down their liquid song of joy and freedom.

"What is it today, then?" asked Dad, appearing behind them. "Birdwatching or boating?"

"Both, if we can arrange it," said Lucy.

"You bet we can," said Sam. "We must go and see the poet."

"I think he'd prefer to be called Mister Baxter," said Dad, "and he probably won't want to be disturbed too early by you two, up with the larks."

"Literally," smiled Lucy.

"But he did say we could go in his boat," persisted Sam.

"Oh yes," said Dad, "I'm sure we will."

"I liked him, but there's something sad about him," remarked Lucy as they prepared breakfast. "I wonder what it is?"

"I thought he was going to be boring," said Sam, "but he's not boring."

"Nobody is really boring once you get to know lots of things about them," Lucy told him.

"Nobody is boring if they have a boat."

There was further discussion as to how and when they should approach the poet, but their plans became pointless when the short fat figure of the poet himself was seen walking through the dunes towards their house. He was wearing white trousers with what looked like tennis shoes and a bush hat. A red scarf was knotted in gypsy style around his neck.

"He looks like a shabby cricketer," observed Dad.

"He wouldn't get on my team," added Sam.

"Stop being nasty about him." Lucy was brushing her hair and preparing to greet the poet. "I like him and I know he's going to be special to us."

"He'll be special when he takes us in that boat," stated Sam.

"That's enough now," said Dad. "Good morning, Mister Baxter!"

"Good morning to all of you!" The poet came up to the front door, breathing rather heavily as if he had exerted himself climbing steep paths through the dunes. "A fine morning again."

"Good morning, Mister Baxter," said the children politely.

"Call me Harry, please," he smiled. "'Mister' is for my students, my dentist, and my bank manager--and I'm very glad to say I shan't be talking to any of them today."

"Would you like breakfast?" offered Lucy. She thought she wouldn't call him 'Harry' just yet. Anyway, he was--and always would be--'the poet'.

"That's very kind of you--but I've just finished mine, thanks. What I really came to say was I think we'd better make this boat trip this morning before the wind increases. It could be much stronger this afternoon."

"Right," said Dad.

"There's only a gentle swell out there and it looks safe enough," continued the poet, "but with four aboard the little boat we don't want it too choppy."

"That's very considerate of you," said Dad.

"So, if you're all ready, we'll have our trip round the bay."

There was a general scamper to collect hats, sunglasses, waterproof jackets, and the binoculars. Then they closed the door of Skylark House and followed the poet down the beach.

"I think we'll just row around the island," he explained. "There are some interesting views from the seaward side; then back to the village anchorage and lunch at the pub, perhaps."

"Oh yes," remembered Dad. "The Ship Inn."

"That's right. Good crab and salmon sandwiches. Watch out for Puffins on the way, and Eiders and Guillemots. We might even see a seal."

"Great!" said Sam.

They were led to a cleft in the dunes directly below Poet's House. There, well hidden among the marram grass, they saw a small rowing boat. Lucy took Sam's arm and pointed at the boat's stern.

"Look," she gasped. "You were right about this place. Now it really is Albatross Bay."

There, in white letters, was the boat's name: *Albatross*.

"She's a considerably less elegant mover than the bird," complained the poet as he and Dad pulled the surprisingly heavy

Albatross down the sand. Some paint flaked off in their hands. "You'd be surprised how much maintenance this little tub needs. There's always something to fix on a boat; always something to worry about. In fact, you could say this one's been hanging round my neck for years."

"That's a real poet's joke," explained Dad.

"We know, we know," answered Lucy, helping Sam with the oars. "We've read *The Rime of the Ancient Mariner*."

"Have we?" asked Sam.

"Of course we have: the famous poem about the sailor who shoots an albatross, has it hung round his neck, then gets into terrible trouble. I've read it, anyway." Lucy turned to the poet. "You're not a re-incarnation of Samuel Taylor Coleridge, are you?"

"Not quite," laughed the poet.

With *Albatross* now at the water's edge, sand was washing off her timbers and she looked a smart little boat. The oars were fitted into the rowlocks which the poet had produced from his pocket, and she was pushed into the waves breaking gently on this part of the beach. Everyone got their feet wet clambering aboard and it was quickly apparent how small she really was when four passengers needed to find seats. Dad and the poet sat together amidships and each took an oar. They looked, as Dad put it, like very well-fed galley slaves. Sam was installed in the tiny seat at the bow. Lucy was last to board, wading out until she had pushed the boat into deeper water and the waves were nearly reaching her shorts; then she hauled herself over the stern, folding her wet legs as best she could so as not to interfere with the rowers.

"All aboard?" asked the poet.

"Yes," called Sam.

"Yes," said Lucy. "A bit wet."

"But an expert boatswoman if you ask me," declared the poet. "That was a very smooth launch. Right, we're off. Steady in the bow there, Sam."

The men pulled on the oars and in moments *Albatross* was through the first big waves and into the open sea. At once they were aware of a bigger swell than they had imagined from the beach. The sea came at them in great grey humps and swilled right up to the boat's gunwales.

"Are you sure we're going to be all right with this weight aboard?" asked Dad.

"We'll be fine," the poet assured them, "as long as we row gently and nobody moves about. Keep an eye out for any big waves,

Lucy, and we'll take them bow-on. Don't worry, we won't be swamped. Now then, Lucy, are we heading straight out past the island?"

"Looks like it."

"Right," he said to Dad. "We just keep going."

The two men rowed easily and well. The island seemed to creep alongside like a huge boat itself, and their perspective of the whole bay was altered with almost every stroke.

"I'd like to take you out far enough to give you a tremendous view," explained the poet. "Almost there now. Tell us what you see to the North, Sam."

Sam looked up the coast.

"There's the Watch House on the point there," he replied, "and a little bay round the point, much smaller than this one.....it's like a pirates' cove.....and there's a big yellow beach coming into view beyond that."

"That's right," said the poet. "We'll keep going."

He and Dad continued to pull on the oars.

"Oh yes!" cried Sam. "There's a huge castle, a great square castle on a hill....."

"That's Bamburgh."

".....then another castle, miles away up the coast.....and islands with lighthouses.....and hills in the distance. It's fantastic!"

"It certainly is," smiled the poet. "Those are the Farne Islands, where the grey seals live, and the other castle is on the holy island of Lindisfarne, and the hills are beyond Berwick, right up in Scotland. Bamburgh is popularly supposed to be Sir Launcelot's castle of Joyous Garde, where he took his beloved Queen Guinevere--until King Arthur marched up with his army and wanted her back."

Now the rowers stopped and they could all admire the wild sweep of coastline and castles, beaches and islands. Little *Albatross* sat low in the water but rode the swell safely enough if everyone sat still-- and everyone did, awestruck by the blue vastness and beautiful views in every direction.

"It's wonderful," said Lucy. "Thank you Mister.....I mean Harry."

"Glad you like it. We'll make back round the island now."

"Look!" Sam pointed out two white birds diving sharply into the sea. "Terns!"

"Lovely birds," said the poet. "Sea Swallows. Look at their forked tails."

They began to learn that the sea, like the land, could show many different faces within a small distance. Here it was suddenly smooth and oily, giving the impression that it would be possible to look straight down at a sandy sea-bed to rocks and wrecks if they happened to be there, although it was actually impossible to see anywhere near the bottom at this depth. Only a few yards away from the boat, patches of turbulent water looked like ploughed fields; further out, waves and swell seemed to stretch into open ocean. Suddenly flashing over a smooth, dark field of water, came a group of fast-flying, smartly-coloured birds, their brightest markings on their heavy bills.

"Puffins," said Sam excitedly. "I love Puffins."

"Off home to the Farne Islands," explained the poet.

Now he and Dad were rowing the boat behind the island, where the wind and the swell were noticeably greater. *Albatross* rose and fell as big seas came in from the horizon, ready to crash against the island or carry on past it to break as waves on the distant beach. Everyone was reminded to keep their seats. Lucy and Sam grasped the gunwales as the vast blue waters rolled under them.

"Are you okay up there, Sam?" Lucy looked between the men at her brother riding the bow seat like the saddle of a unpredictable pony.

"Of course," he reported. "It's great up here."

"No changing seats now," warned Dad.

"No Gannets today," the poet was searching the horizon. "There's a big colony on the Bass Rock. That's a long way to the North, but you do sometimes see them down here. No seals coming round the boat today, either--but keep a look out for them."

Lucy and Sam looked for seals, but were really remembering their encounter with the woman on the rocks of the island. The very place where they had seen her was sliding past on their port side as Dad and the poet rowed *Albatross* Northwards, intending to make a wide sweep back to the beach at the village end of the bay. Out here, they felt remote from the land, low down amid swelling water stetching away to nothing. It was suddenly lonely, far from the beach and their cosy cottage. Even in this fair Summer weather there was a hint of cold seas and shipwrecks, big waves and helpless drownings, strange fish and mermaids--and not the kind you met on holiday who were actually real women able to dive brilliantly in elegant swimsuits, but the kind found in frightening stories and cruel legends. Lucy--who was a good swimmer herself and not afraid of the sea--began to feel vulnerable in this tiny boat and thought a lifejacket would have been a good idea, but since everyone else appeared to be enjoying the trip so much she wasn't going to say so. Anyway, she guessed they would be in safer waters very soon, as Dad and the poet were already swinging *Albatross's* bow towards the shore. She was just beginning to think about lunch and what kind of sandwiches they might order when a head rose up from the water not ten yards off their starboard bow.

"That's not a seal!" shouted Sam. "That's the mermaid!"

The head shook water from its short blonde curls and a suntanned arm came up to wave at them. The poet waved back.

"That's not a mermaid," he laughed, "that's Sue."

It seemed incredible that so exotic a creature could have so simple a name--but Lucy and Sam guessed Sue must be short for Susan or even Susannah, surely more of a mermaid's name than Sue. Yet Sue was a sweet and friendly name; out here in the wild seas it somehow made the haughty swimmer more lovable.

"You might be right of course," the poet was saying with a chuckle still in his voice. "She's as close as you'll get to a mermaid round here, or anywhere. She's an ocean-going swimmer, that one."

"You know her?" Sam still couldn't quite believe it.

"Oh yes. She has the other cottage in the dunes."

"What--the little wooden house along from us, even smaller than ours?"

"That's the one."

"We're meeting all the neighbours," remarked Dad, wide-eyed, "even those we didn't know we had."

Since no-one was being polite enough to greet her properly, Lucy thought she should be the first to speak to the mermaid and shouted "Hello!" across the water, waving at the same time. The head went under rapidly--seeming to confirm the children's original impression of a rude and unfriendly woman--only to re-surface much nearer the boat. Water streamed from her face as she blinked open bright blue eyes. The children knew her skin was suntanned, but here, submerged in cold water, her body looked pale--and didn't appear to be wearing a swimsuit. She spoke through very white teeth glinting in the sunshine.

"Hello again." Lucy was amazed this woman wasn't breathless after swimming so far in rough seas. The voice came as languidly as if they had been chatting over a tea table. Then, quite unexpectedly, the curly head turned to face Dad and spoke in much harsher tones. "You must be the father of these two."

"Hello. Yes, I am." Dad sounded a little flustered at this unusual encounter.

"Well you might keep a better eye on them round here." The voice was haughty and displeased. "Did you know they were scrambling about on the island unaware of the tide and current?"

"Er--yes," replied Dad, perplexed. "But my children are actually very sensible."

"Good thing they are, with so many careless adults about." Before Dad could make any reply she had turned to the poet. "And you ought to know better than to go out in a sea like this with four people in that pathetic boat. You've got no more than a handsbreadth freeboard in this swell."

"We'll be all right, Sue," answered the poet with a strange smile, "and you should mind your manners with these good people."

"It's the children's safety I'm concerned about," she went on undaunted. "I'm sure they're very nice children and I want them to have a good holiday, not suffer some tragedy brought about by silly and stubborn men!"

"Now go on with you," chuckled the poet. "We'll be all right. You want to watch the current yourself. You're a long way out here. You wouldn't want to be swept ashore in Berwick dressed like that."

"Oh!" she snapped. "Men!"

With that she slipped below the waves. They all watched the pale body surge away powerfully under the water.

"Built like a torpedo," said Dad, "and almost as explosive."

"Was she really swimming like a proper mermaid," asked Sam. "I mean with nothing on?"

"Nothing on her top half, anyway," laughed the poet, "but she's no dresser at the best of times. Plenty of money, they say, and from a good family, but she comes up here to get away from them and wears nothing but rags."

"She had a very smart swimsuit on last time," answered Lucy.

"She obviously keeps her best for the sea, then," smiled the poet, "or thinks her own skin is the smartest outfit of all. I reckon she loves the sea more than anything. On land, she's in raggy tousers and jumpers you wouldn't keep for gardening; never wears shoes. They call her 'Barefoot Sue' in the village."

"But it's nice not to wear shoes," said Lucy, wiggling her own bare toes. "Mermaids shouldn't wear shoes, anyway."

"I think she's strange," Sam told the poet, "but she is beautiful. Don't you think so?"

"Many a man would say she's beautiful indeed."

"What do you think of her, Dad?" asked Lucy. "Don't you think she's a beautiful lady?"

"She might be beautiful but I'm not sure she's a lady," replied Dad. "She's certainly got some cheek."

"Well I think she's rather wonderful," said Lucy wistfully. "I wish I could swim like that, and look like that when I'm older, but I know I never will."

Why did grown-ups always have to laugh at her special thoughts?

"You wouldn't want all your lovely hair cut off to frizzy little curls like that, would you?" grinned the poet.

Lucy smiled back at him then looked out to sea. The mermaid's head was visible again, golden against the dark water, rising up and down with the swell beside her rocks. No, she thought, she did not want her own hair so short, but she did want to be beautiful and lithe and proud and carefree and grown-up in the way that woman was; wearing rags if she wanted to, swimming like a mermaid, living her own life in a cottage by the sea. If she couldn't be like that just yet, then she wanted to meet her again and somehow become friends with her; somehow--and she couldn't think how--make her part of her own family. That didn't seem very likely, and as the boat neared the village, Lucy stopped wondering how and when she might see her again, and started wondering what would be for lunch at the Ship Inn.

Chapter 7   At the Ship Inn

Albatross was rowed steadily towards the shore, and in a few minutes was grounding on the beach. Lucy and Sam splashed into the water, helping to pull the boat up the sand, this time below the cluster of houses and the Ship Inn.

Lucy's thoughts returned to the mermaid, now surely far away on the distant shore of her island. Would it feel good to wear ragged clothes and go barefoot all day: in and out of the water, across the grass, through the village to the shop, feeling the hot rocks and the damp sand and everything else under your toes? Would it really be fun to live away from the family, put on your smartest swimsuit only for going in the empty sea, swim far from everybody and sit lonely on a rock? There was good and bad in it, thought Lucy; something strange, but something fascinating. Then she and Sam quickly became more fascinated by the prospect of lunch at a real seaside inn, perhaps once the haunt of smugglers and pirates.

Outside, the Ship Inn had old barrels and ship's planking made into seats; inside, it had delicious smells of hot buns, pickles and pies, and the much-anticipated crab and salmon sandwiches. Never mind strange women who may or may not be mermaids, now there were decisions to be made about which sandwiches to have--and should it be tea or orange juice, home-made scones or ginger biscuits?

Lucy and Sam could see that Dad and Harry Baxter were becoming good friends. The poet was telling Dad about the Viking raids which had been made along this coast centuries ago and pointing out one of the Northumbrian cobles riding at anchor in this part of the bay, explaining they were seagoing fishing boats derived from Viking ships. Lucy and Sam could certainly recognise a curved hull and high prow similar to pictures of Viking ships they had seen in books. Dad was suggesting that the poet should have named his boat after one of the Norse goddesses rather than call it *Albatross*, but the poet said it was bad luck to change a boat's name. She had been *Albatross* when he had bought her and *Albatross* she would stay, and Lucy and Sam were happy with that.

The talk turned to fishing expeditions and birdwatching walks and the poet was promising to take them to the lake when he came back.

"Are you going away then?" queried Sam.

"Yes." The poet was already getting up from the table and collecting his things. "I have to go back to my College for a few days, but I'll be here again next week. Take *Albatross* out whenever you like. I'll leave you the rowlocks."

"That's very generous of you," said Dad.

"Not in heavy seas, of course," warned the poet. "You've already seen what she's like in a swell. She's really just for pottering about inside the bay here, and," he turned to Lucy and Sam, "you two must promise to pull her right back up the beach and tie her up in her proper place under my house. You can keep the oars and rowlocks in your own cottage so no-one can steal her."

"We promise," said Lucy and Sam, and the poet left them amid many 'goodbyes' and 'thank yous'.

Lucy and Sam sat with Dad at the window of the inn, looking over the bay, watching white spray fly off more and more waves as the offshore wind strengthened through the afternoon, just as the poet had said it would. It brought clouds over the hills and piled them up together in the first threatening sky they had seen since their arrival.

"Too rough for swimming now," Dad decided out loud. "I thought we might go in today, but look at it: definitely too rough."

'Except for mermaids,' thought Lucy, but didn't say so.

"And I've eaten too much for swimming anyway," confessed Sam.

"I think we were lucky to get back without any trouble," continued Dad. "Four people in that little boat really wasn't a good idea."

"But you rowed us home safely," said Sam.

"Yes--and look at these muscles," grinned Dad, "aching like mad. Lucky we're not Vikings, having to sail and row all the way from Norway."

"In worse weather than this," added Sam.

"So how about a look around this little village?" offered Dad. "The we can walk back along the beach and make ourselves a cosy supper while the wind and weather do whatever they like outside."

"We love our cosy suppers, Dad," Lucy smiled, "and thanks for a great time so far."

"There might be a real storm," said Sam, stepping into the wind. Even as far inland as the front of the inn, stinging sand was being whipped around his legs.

"There might be," agreed Dad.

Chapter 8   The Mermaid comes Ashore

It was a windy walk back along the beach, clouds racing up from the South West, pale streams of dry sand snaking along at knee height and spattering the children's legs. All the time a new, loud, angry sound came from the sea as the wind thrashed increasing waves into one another and white-rolling breakers smashed on to the sand with a ferocity they had not seen before.

"It's a real storm now!" Sam shouted into the wind.

"It certainly is," replied Dad, "but at least it's a Summer storm: no freezing rain or solid cloud. Look at those clouds racing over the sun."

"It's not even really cold, is it?" said Lucy. "Just windy. If we're going to have a storm I'm glad it's a Summer storm."

"It must be really wild up here in the Winter," remarked Dad.

"If we had a barometer," said Sam, always interested in science, "I wonder what it would be doing."

"Going down," stated Lucy.

"What the old sailors called 'a falling glass'," explained Dad. "Bad weather sucked into low pressure, rough seas, battening down hatches."

"It'll be great to watch a real storm, safe and dry in our cottage," said Sam, "like being on a wooden ship riding high above the waves."

"Without having to be seasick," added Lucy.

Back at Skylark House they indeed 'battened down hatches': putting extra ropes across the motorcycle cover, closing the front door firmly, making sure all the windows were shut tightly. Even so, the wind found its way under the door, around the window frames, and between gaps in the wooden-planked walls they had not noticed before. They felt snug and safe enough inside, but as they prepared their supper the wind increased again and there was constant noise from the thrashing of the marram grass in the dunes, the rattling of the windows, the spatter of sand against the glass, and the deeper, more distant thunder of the sea. The weather might be turning savage, but its noises were all sounds of Nature in perfect harmony with the wild beauty of the place.....until they were disturbed by a very human knocking on the door.

When Dad opened it they were amazed to see Sue. She could no longer be called 'the mermaid' with any conviction. Now her short curls were bright and dry and she was wearing a pale blue jersey; she had transformed herself into a woman of the land. For all that, she still looked exotic with flashing teeth and glowing skin--and with canvas trousers cut roughly above her suntanned ankles and shoeless feet she was indeed the ragged 'Barefoot Sue' of the poet's description.

"Come to apologise," she said immediately in her surprisingly deep voice before anyone could welcome her or ask what she wanted. "I might have seemed rather sharp and rude. Didn't mean to be; I was just concerned about the children's welfare. The coast is magnificent here, but the sea can be very dangerous."

"You'll be all right." Sam was unexpectedly the first to reply. "You're an expert swimmer; underwater, too. How long can you stay under? You're great!"

"Well," their strange, tall visitor smiled down at him, "I've had a lot of experience--and that's how I know everyone has to be careful about the tides and currents."

"Yes of course," Dad found his voice at last. "We.....er.....we appreciate what you've done."

"All I've done is snap at you," came the blunt reply.

"Well.....er....." Dad was still being flustered, but Lucy could see he was beginning to melt under the blue stare that held them all fascinated. "I think we'll forgive you. Not that there's really anything to forgive."

"Right." She extended a long arm in a rather masculine way and gave them all firm handshakes. "Friends then."

"Friends," they all said.

"You must come in, out of this wind," said Dad, but Sue did not move.

"I actually wanted to be friends with you from the very start." Lucy hoped her admission would bring Sue inside.

"Really? That's very nice."

Dad introduced them all as politely as he could while holding the door in the vicious wind.

"I'm Sue. Just Sue when I live here."

"Does that mean you have another name when you live somewhere else?" queried Sam.

"Just Sue," she repeated, silencing all questions with another blue stare.

"Look," said Dad, "you must come in. Please join us for supper."

Lucy thought he was never going to ask.

"Sorry, can't. There's.....er.....there's something on the stove back at the house. Very kind of you though."

"Another time then, perhaps," said Dad.

"Perhaps. Goodbye." She strode away on her bare feet, the wind snatching her clothes and hair. "Watch that canvas motorbike cover in this gale. I like bikes. You can show me over it sometime."

"Certainly. Goodbye."

Dad shut the door, swirls of sand settling on the floor.

"I was going to ask her if she *ever* wears shoes," said Sam.

"You've asked quite enough already, young man," said Dad sternly. "If she has a blunt manner we needn't be impertinent in return."

"I like her," confessed Lucy. "I think she's shy. That's what makes her sound rude. She's a mermaid who's found herself on dry land and she can't get used to ordinary people."

"I wonder what she's cooking on her own stove," said Sam.

"It would be nice to make her supper here one night, don't you think?" Lucy was setting out their dishes. "Just once, so we could get more friendly."

"Yes," said Dad, "if she'd like that."

"If we get that friendly," decided Sam as he put out the biscuits, "she can teach me to swim like a mermaid."

"Only you'd have to swim like a mer*man*," observed Lucy.

They ate around the table in front of the stove, for although it was not cold, the lashing wind and thundering sea were wintry sounds and they were glad to feel snug in their small wooden room. The wind had brought more solid cloud to replace the scudding drifts; the sun was obscured and the evening grew dark much earlier than on the fair Summer nights they had enjoyed until now.

After supper Dad went out to check the motorbike cover once more and returned to close the door tightly and secure all the windows again. Sam sat at the table making a bigger version of his map. Lucy went to the bathroom, brushed as much windblown sand out of her hair as she could, and found even more to shake out of her clothes. Then they sat at the stove for a while, talking about what had happened, but they all felt tired after their long and eventful day and went to their bedrooms before it was completely dark.

It was difficult to settle down to sleep with the wind thrashing outside, dashing sand against the windows, and creaking the roof and planks of the cottage all around them.

"It really is like being on a ship," said Sam. "I can feel my bunk heaving in the waves.....waves of wind, of course, not water. You're not asleep, are you?"

"Of course I'm not asleep," answered Lucy from the other bunk. "How could anyone sleep in all this noise?"

"Sailors must be able to."

"I've still got sand in my hair," Lucy grumbled. "It's horrible. I'll have to wash it properly tomorrow."

"If you cut your hair off and just had little curls like the mermaid it wouldn't be a problem."

"If I cut my hair that short it wouldn't go into curls, it would just be straight and spikey and I'd look terrible."

"D'you think she really does have another name? D'you think she's hiding here, pretending to be someone else? D'you think she's a spy?"

"I don't think so, Sam." Lucy was trying to make herself more comfortable without sounding too annoyed by silly ideas. "Now let's go to sleep."

"But I'm not sleepy. I'm listening to the storm. The roof's moving--I'm sure it is. Shall we tell Dad?"

"No, Sam. He might be asleep. We'll be all right now. Turn over and get comfy if you can."

They stopped talking, but could not stop thinking. Lucy thought how good it would be to wake up to a proper Summer's day again with no wind or crashing waves, wash her hair, and put on a clean blouse and shorts that weren't full of scratchy sand. If it was warm enough she might go all day without shoes, like 'Barefoot Sue'. What a strange woman she was, with her short, sharp words and almost angry eyes--but they were beautiful eyes, too, thought Lucy. She was beautiful all over, with that wonderfully suntanned skin. It would be great to be real friends with her, and learn to swim like that.....so long as Sam wasn't rude or silly and didn't say things to annoy her and make the fragile friendship difficult to preserve. But of course she would understand Sam was a boy, growing up. She would understand everything. She might be some brilliant student on Summer vacation, or perhaps a businesswoman escaping her city life, hiding away in her little house, swimming all day, not talking to people if she didn't want to but knowing everything about life and understanding it. That would be wonderful, thought Lucy: to be smart and grown-up and free and wild in that way. Sam mustn't spoil it. She wouldn't let him. Was he asleep yet?

Sam wasn't asleep, but he was pretending to be. He was thinking how difficult it must be to swim under water--but then if a tall, fully-grown woman like Sue could do it, he should be able to do it even better, once he was taught the techniques of holding his breath and using his hands like the planes of a submarine to keep his body under. Of course Sue wasn't a mermaid, she was a real woman who was applying scientific knowledge to swim that way. She was a real woman, but not quite an ordinary woman. In fact, decided Sam, she wasn't ordinary at all.

At last the wind seemed to subside a little, or perhaps they had just grown accustomed to its noise, and dreams began to overtake their thoughts. Lucy began to dream she was in a Viking ship skimming over bright blue seas, and there stood Sue in the prow, her golden head in the sun. She reached down into the boat and drew up a great green cloak which billowed in the wind. She put it round Lucy and put another one round herself and fastened them with golden brooches and they were both Viking princesses standing at the dragon's head prow, looking over the white waves to Norway. Sam began to dream he was rowing *Albatross* quite easily and safely, riding the dark blue swell to a kind of music, haunting and beautiful but with no particular tune, music he had never heard before but wanted to hear for ever. Up and down rode the little boat, softly and sweetly, and there in the sea was Sue's golden head. She was a mermaid again, lifted by the swell in time to the music and the boat, smiling at him across the water. She was beautiful. She was very beautiful. When he was old enough he would fall in love with her, but for now they would just be friends, and go swimming whenever she said the tides and currents were right.....and the right tides and currents seemed to sweep over him and he was asleep again and not dreaming--at least not dreaming anything he could remember.

Chapter 9   The Storm

There was a crash over their heads as something hit the roof and a crash in front of them as Dad burst through their bedroom door.

"Did you hear that?" he shouted. "Are you all right?"

"What was it, Dad? Are *you* all right?"

Lucy and Sam tumbled out of their beds, completely awake in moments, and aware once more of the wind thrashing around the cottage--only now it was much more savage. It was racing across the dunes in great gusts and coming at them like the hand-slaps of a furious giant.

"Is the window smashed?" yelled Sam.

"Are the walls breaking down?" cried Lucy.

"No," said Dad. "It's the roof. Listen."

They did not have to wait long before the next gust of wind hit them with the noise of an express train. It blasted against the house, straining every joint, creaking every plank, and thrashing something loose, dangerously close above their heads.

"The roof's coming off!" Sam was wide-eyed.

"I think it's just the felt," said Dad. "It's torn off and flapping about. The planks are still on, but the wind's getting under the roof where it joins the walls and it could be dangerous. We'd better get dressed and stay together in the main room."

"Okay," said Sam, struggling into his clothes.

"Is the motorbike all right?" asked Lucy.

"So far."

"Lucky we parked it in the lee of the house," said Sam.

"If the house stays up," said Lucy.

In a few moments they were all dressed and gathered in the main room, where the wind was rattling the stove-pipe and seemed to have dislodged the front door. Sand could be seen blowing in around the frame. They were suddenly aware of a strange brightness--and realised the heavy cloud had gone to reveal dazzling moonlight with only a few rags of cloud tearing across an indgo sky.

"The sea looks amazing!" cried Sam, looking out of the window. "It's completely white--in the middle of the night."

"Don't say we've got another poet," joked Dad.

"Are we going to be all right?" Lucy looked up at the ceiling. "Is the house really going to blow down?"

"I don't think so," said Dad, "but something might break off the roof. We must be careful not to get hurt, so we'll stay together."

"Should we get ready to run outside?" asked Sam, pulling on a woolly hat.

"Not if we can avoid it," grinned Dad.

"But shouldn't we take a look?" Sam went on. "We could see if the bike's all right. We could look at the moonlight on the sea. It looks like boiling water."

"Okay--but I'll hold the door. Are we ready?"

Dad opened the door with both hands. He had to push it open as if two or three giants were trying to stop him, then he had to hold it back as if two or three giants were trying to snatch it out of his hands. His hair and shirt were blown round his head.

"Just a quick look!" he shouted, and the children stepped towards the wild night, holding on to the door frame. They were ready to admire the brilliant moonlight, to be awed by the sight of the boiling sea, to be rather frightened by the creak and sway of the house, to be anxious about what was happening to their roof--but they did none of these things. Instead, they watched in fascinated horror as pieces of wood and cloth and paper and board came flying past their door and were blown down to the beach.

"Oh no!" yelled Dad. "It's the other house. It's Sue's house. Look!"

They looked--and saw the wooden cottage, only a few yards from their own, actually swaying in the wind. Its roof had come off and was lying in pieces on the sand-streaked grass. Long gusts of wind were sucking and lifting what looked like wreckage out of the roofless walls, as if monstrous unseen hands were reaching into a big box and throwing out unwanted rubbish. Pieces of cloth which might have been clothes or bedding had caught on the planks; others had blown away down the dunes. Sue herself appeared: a tall figure, pale in the moonlight. At one moment she seemed to be dodging the gusts behind the remains of her house; at another, trying to hold up a swaying wall; at another, hopelessly chasing a box which had been snatched away by the gale. It was like watching a slow-motion film of a nightmare.

"Come on!" shouted Dad. "We must help her!"

They all staggered out to face the wind, Dad slamming their own door shut behind them.

"Be careful now," he shouted. "We'll help her, but we must look after ourselves. If you think you're going to be blown over, sit down straight away--and watch out for anything flying towards us. Got that?"

"We understand, Dad." Lucy took Sam's hand.

"We're coming to save you!" shouted Sam.....and they all hurried across the uneven ground as fast as they could, the wild roaring of the sea in their ears, the howl of the wind against their bodies, sand blowing into their squinting eyes, thin clouds scudding over the moon to make shadows race across the blue and silver night.

It was like swimming through chill water or trying to stand upright in some crazily careering vehicle; like facing a shower of needles or standing too close to a train passing at full speed. At last they struggled up to Sue. Dad put an arm around her.

"Are you all right?" he shouted as she looked at him with an expression Lucy and Sam had never seen before: a woman frightened and defiant at the same time, relieved and frustrated, half-way between fury and tears. They expected her to tear herself away from Dad, but for a few moments she seemed to rest in his strong arms and they knew she was suddenly happy to be encircled by them and that she felt safe being held against his chest. Then she did squirm and he let her out of his grasp, but kept holding one of her hands.

"Yes, I'm all right," she said, "but look at this mess. Look at it! I'll be ruined. There'll be nothing left. I'm finished. Finished!"

They saw she was almost crying--then suddenly was not going to cry, full of hard resolve, yet empty of hope.

"No you're not," said Dad. "You'll be all right. You're safe now. Come on--you must come away from here in case the whole thing collapses. You'll stay with us. Come on."

They saw her realise, against her will, that she had to allow Dad to lead her away. They were all blown back to the door of Skylark House, which Dad opened hurriedly. They staggered inside and Dad shut out the storm. Chaos subsided around them, but Dad kept hold of the door knob as if ready to go out again.

"Is there anything you need desperately from over there?"

"No," Sue shook her head. "No thanks. We'll see what's left in the morning. You.....you've been very kind," she added with a shake in her voice, running her hands through her hair in the same gesture Lucy and Sam had first seen when she had been sitting on her rock--only now she wasn't the mysterious mermaid, she was a real woman standing right next to them, and she was consumed by rising anger.

"You'll be all right," Dad re-assured her.

"We'll help you," said Sam.

"You can stay with us," said Lucy. "We really do want you to stay and be safe here."

She forced a kind of smile at them, then they saw her clench her brown hands into fists and stamp a bare foot on the floor.

"To be beaten," she growled in a tense fury. "To be beaten.....by the wind, of all things, by just the wind!"

Dad held out a hand to her.

"We'll help you put your house right," he said gently.

"We'll re-build it if we have to," ventured Sam. "We'll make it stronger than ever for you."

"You don't understand," she was on the verge of tears again, "you have no idea what this place means to me....."

"I think we do," said Dad, now holding out both arms.

She made no move to take his hands in friendship or find a safe haven in his arms, which Lucy knew he was offering. She scowled at the door and clenched her fists again, which Sam knew was a danger signal.

"It's not fair!" she exploded. "It's not fair! I've done so much here, been here so long, thought everything was my friend: the sea, the island, the sky.....and now the wind has to kill me.....just the wind....." She was sobbing now and hid her face in her hands. "Just the wind.....such a simple thing....." She had suddenly gone into Dad's arms and he was saying nothing, just holding her. "I was going.....to do so much more here....." She was wiping her face, streaks of tears under her fingers. "Do so much more.....be so happy....."

"You will be," said Dad.

Lucy and Sam were going to say the same but Dad looked at them over Sue's curly head now buried against his chest.

"Let's make another supper," said Lucy instead. "You help me, Sam. Come on."

They heard Sue straighten up and say: "I'm sorry--this is ridiculous. You must think I'm mad."

"I think you're lucky to get over here uninjured," Dad was being sensible again and showing her into the bathroom. "I wouldn't have liked to be in there when that roof came off. We thought ours was coming off a while ago."

"I'm glad it didn't." Sue sounded as if she was drying her eyes. "I think the storm's abating a bit now. Done enough damage, but I think the worst is over."

"I know it is," said Dad. "You will stay overnight, won't you?"

"Think I'll have to." Lucy and Sam heard a faint chuckle in Sue's voice, and knew the crisis was over. "It's enormously kind of you."

"Not at all," they heard Dad say. "Would you mind sharing the bedroom with Lucy? Sam can move in with me."

"Of course--whatever you like. I'll go anywhere. I'll try not to make a nuisance of myself."

"You couldn't possibly be a nuisance."

"Oh yes I could," came her jokey reply, "but I promise to behave. I owe you another apology for making a fool of myself just now."

"It's perfectly understandable," Dad was saying. "You've had a nasty shock and every reason to be upset. Nobody thinks your a fool."

"Nobody here, perhaps," she answered. "Anyway, you've been very kind to me already. Thank you."

Despite the terrors of the storm--which did indeed seem to be passing--it was enormously exciting for Lucy and Sam to have Sue right here in their own house. Here she was: the mermaid, the brusque and unconventional neighbour, the ragged and exotic beachcomber, the proud and haughty swimmer, the frightened girl and angry woman, right here with all her mystery and beauty, talking to Dad in the next room--and going to stay!

"We all think you're very special," Dad was saying quietly. "The kids are most impressed."

"Are they? I hope I've made the *right* impression for once. I'm famous for getting people's backs up. I'll explain some time. I'll tell you the story.....some time.....about my house here and everything."

"I'd really like to hear it." That was Dad's kindest voice.

"Yes, well," Sue had brightened again, "some time." They could hear her brushing her trousers and straightening her jersey. "I must look like an explosion in a sand-pit."

"Anything but." There was a smile in Dad's voice. "You do look as if you'd be expelled from Roedean, though."

Lucy and Sam heard the new--but very welcome--sound of laughter.

"What's Roedean?" whispered Sam.

"A posh school."

"Did she go there?"

"Possibly. It's a joke."

"What does it mean?"

"It means they're all right," said Lucy. "Come on, this is ready now."

"Midnight feast," announced Sam, presenting the first dishes as everyone met together again. "Scrambled egg on toast."

During second supper--or was it more of a first breakfast?--there was much talk of what they would do when the storm died down the next day, and what they would do about extra bedding now.

"I'll just bed down as I am," said Sue.

"No, you can't," said Lucy. "You'll have my extra blanket."

"Over my sleeping-bag," added Sam.

"No," protested Sue.

"Yes," said Dad, looking stern. "Sam will manage with my flying-jacket as a pillow."

"Like a cowboy with his saddle," grinned Sam.

"You can borrow my other pyjamas," offered Lucy.

"She's too big," Sam insisted loudly. "She'll have to borrow Dad's other pyjamas."

"I think we should let a lady decide herself what she's going to sleep in, Sam." Dad looked embarrassed and annoyed at the same time.

"Really," Sue rescued the situation with a smile, "I'll manage as I am."

A new bed was made up for Sam in Dad's room, and Lucy re-arranged Sam's bunk for Sue.

"You've made it a very comfortable cabin," she told Lucy.

"Not exactly First Class on the *Queen Mary*," said Lucy, stowing her clothes and bags to make it tidier, "more like a girls' dormitory."

"I've slept in much worse. This is very cosy. Oh," she added with surprise as she sat on what had been Sam's bunk, "and very comfy."

"We sleep *in* the bags on Winter trips and *on* them in the Summer. They make good mattresses."

"You've been very kind," said Sue again. "This must be a tremendous bother for you."

"It's a bit of excitement, to be honest," admitted Lucy. "Not for you, of course."

"It's excitement I could have done without," said Sue ruefully. "My little house here is very precious to me.....or rather it was."

Lucy thought she was ready to cry again.

"We'll re-build it for you. Dad's brilliant at that kind of thing."

"We'll see what can be done," smiled Sue. "At least, if my house has blown down, I have made new friends."

"Yes." Lucy was delighted to take the outstretched hands she had not expected Sue to offer. "I know we're going to be very special friends. We'll sort everything out in the morning. You can hear the wind's dropping already."

"Yes," said Sue. "I'm exhausted now. I'll try to sleep."

She rolled herself under the blanket, her tall figure filling the bunk, her golden head strange and beautiful on the pillow. The most powerful gusts of wind had stopped, but there was still a moaning and creaking around the house. The sea boomed incessantly upon the beach, but a new calm had settled in the little bedroom. Lucy thought Sue might be asleep already when Dad appeared at the door. He beckoned Lucy quietly into the main room.

"Everything all right in there? She's been very upset, you know. You won't make her talk too much or ask her awkward questions, will you?"

"Of course not, Dad. I'll let her be herself."

"That's my girl."

"You're right, Dad. We do think she's special."

"I know we do. We must treat her very carefully."

"We must treat her with love, mustn't we?"

"Yes, we must. Goodnight."

Chapter 10   After the Storm

When Lucy woke to the sound of early Skylarks, she knew the storm was over. She opened her eyes to bright sunlight and a silence she had almost forgotten. It seemed to fold down from a warm sky over the whole bay and fill the little bedroom with tranquility. Then she turned over and saw the head of bright curls lying on the opposite bunk's pillow--and once more, strange excitements, hopes, and plans slid into her mind.

She swung out of bed as quietly as she could and crept out of the room--only to find Dad and Sam already up and making breakfast. Sunlight streamed through the open door giving its Summer view of golden beach and bright blue sea as if there had never been a storm or a wild night of disaster and surprises.

"She's sleeping late," whispered Lucy.

"I wonder how long she'd been fighting the wind before we rescued her?" asked Sam. "She might want to sleep all day."

"No chance of that!" Sue appeared behind them, dishevelled but smiling. "I hate sleeping late. Thank you all for my good rest. I'll go over to my place for a wash and find some clean clothes."

"You will be back for breakfast?" pleaded Sam.

"I will, thanks."

Lucy was about to offer her their own bathroom and any clothes she might like to borrow, but a look from Dad silenced her and seemed to say 'let her go her own way'. Then Lucy saw another look cross Dad's face that seemed to say 'but please come back'.

* * *

Sue did return, wearing a shirt and jeans and looking freshly washed.

"Amazingly," she announced, "my shower's still working."

"You have a shower?" Sam was impressed. "We just have a tiny bathtub here."

"I swim so much I need one, so I rigged one up myself."

"Underwater swimmer *and* engineering genius," declared Sam. "I want to live in a house with a shower."

"It's not quite habitable yet," Sue told Dad, "but not as bad as I feared--if we can somehow stick the roof back on. As far as I can see, it's come off in two big pieces and neither of them are actually broken."

"We'll put it back on," said Sam. "We'll be a team of builders. I'll work out what size nails and screws we'll need."

"Sam is *our* engineering genius," smiled Dad. "What's it really like over there."

"Bit of a mess inside. To be honest I don't know what I'd do without your help."

"Come on then," Sam was leading them out of the house. "It's a nice day for building work, and no wind."

"I'm pleased to hear that," added Sue. "Be careful not to hurt yourselves on any nails sticking out of splintered wood."

"I love the way you have my children's safety at heart," remembered Dad.

"Pity my own record wasn't better," returned Sue ruefully. "This house wouldn't pass any safety inspection."

"I don't know." Dad was looking around the shattered building. "It really is just the roof. Once that's back on, the whole structure should be rigid again and we'll only need to replace some nails and screws in the planking."

"Told you," grinned Sam. "Have you got a stepladder?"

"You're not going to believe this," smiled Sue, "but yes, I have. I use it for painting jobs and putting up curtains.....which are down on the beach this morning, I think. Everything's going to need a wash."

"Roof on first," said Dad--and they set to work.

Sue's cottage was so small that it was surprisingly easy to lift the roof sections back on. They were big, but not particularly heavy. Everyone helped to slide them into position. Dad ensured they fitted as snugly as possible and climbed on to the roof-ridge to hammer in some nails.

"A roll of felt would finish the job nicely and make it waterproof," he called down, "but that'll be a special order from the town, I suppose. We'll use the old stuff for now."

When he climbed down he found Lucy and Sam eager to go round tightening screws and knocking in nails, so he gave them the hammer and screwdriver.

"Make sure you check them all," he said, "and mind your fingers."

Lucy and Sam started at the door edges and began to work round all the planks.

"That'll keep them busy," said Dad, finding a comfortable place on the sandy grass and inviting Sue to sit beside him. She wound her legs under her in exactly the same way Lucy and Sam had seen when they had known her only as the mermaid on the rock.

"Will they really be all right? This work is a terrible imposition on you."

"No it's not." Lucy and Sam could detect the smile in Dad's voice, although he and Sue seemed to think they couldn't be overheard. "The kids are loving every minute of it."

"I'm beginning to love things again, too," sighed Sue. "I was full of hate and anger last night. I'm sorry I was so ungracious."

"That's perfectly understandable, being angry and hurt by a stroke of bad luck. It was because you love this place so much, wasn't it? D'you want to tell me about it?"

"I do love this place," Sue began. "I love being free here, being my own woman when I need to be. I'm afraid I fell out with my father about not marrying someone he had all set for me."

"Oh, I'm sorry," said Dad. "Aren't arranged marriages rather out-of-date these days?"

"They may be out-of-date, but some fathers still like to arrange them. Mine did anyway, but I wasn't in love with this man, had no intention of marrying him, made other arrangements, and found myself a hideaway. This little house is my private and secret place. That's why I was so angry at losing it."

"You've just got it back," smiled Dad, indicating Lucy and Sam hammering behind them.

"Yes. You've restored me, too. I've been lucky to meet you; not everyone here is as good as you and your family."

"You have trouble with the neighbours?"

"No. My only neighbour is Harry Baxter, the chap you met with the boat. He's no threat to anybody: a rather sad man, I think; very clever too, apparently. No, I meant some visitors here are noisy at week-ends and leave litter on the beach; things like that. I shouldn't really complain, but I get very protective about this place and my quiet life in it."

"Quite right, if you love it."

"I do love it, but not the man I was supposed to marry. I'm a terrible disappointment to my father. 'A grown woman', he says in that imperious voice of his; oh yes, he's very distinguished, 'taller than me and not married.' But I wouldn't marry without love and 'm not in love with anybody. I don't think I can be."

"Oh." Lucy and Sam heard Dad shift and re-settle himself on the grass. "It's amazing how people can fall in love."

"Have you ever been in love?"

There was a pause.

"Oh, I'm sorry," she gasped. "Personal question. I know I'm blunt. I tend to say just what comes into my head."

"Admirable." Dad sounded quite happy about her bluntness. "Yes, I have been in love."

"Of course--with the mother of your children."

"Yes. We were very happy. Then she died in an accident just after Sam was born. He never knew her. I don't think Lucy remembers her either. She was only three."

"It must have been terrible for you; and here was I, crying over a broken roof."

"We've managed very well really," continued Dad. "We make a good little family; a bit hectic sometimes, but there's an added bonus: my children keep me young."

"Married with children," mused Sue. "Doesn't come naturally to me; I can't imagine it. Of course my father imagined it for me. 'If you'd grow your hair and put on some decent clothes you might attract a worthwhile husband instead of living like a hermit in a shack.' That's what he calls me: a hermit in a shack; but he doesn't understand me." She turned her golden head to face Dad directly. "Do you?"

"Yes." Dad had turned to face her, too. "And will you grant us the favour of not doing that, at least not while we're here?"

"Not doing what?"

"Growing your hair and putting on some decent clothes. We like you just as you are."

Lucy and Sam heard quiet laughter.

"And it's not true," Dad was saying. "You are natural with children."

"Just a big kid myself, really."

"Nearly home and dry," said Lucy to Sam.

"But I've still got dozens of nails to do round this side," he answered.

Lucy put down her screwdriver.

"Not the house, silly."

* * *

"That's it then," declared Dad after an inspection of the building work, "apart from the interior decorating, of course." He found a shredded tea-towel in a corner and handed it to Sue.

"We should celebrate," said Sue.

"With a picnic?" said Lucy.

"If you like."

"On the island?" added Sam. "The tide is going down and Dad makes great picnics."

"Can we really have a picnic on your island?"asked Lucy.

"Of course," said Sue. "I'll bring some apples--if I can find them in that mess."

"I'll make the sandwiches," said Dad.

Chapter 11   On the Island

Re-building a house--even a house as small as Sue's--had made for a strenuous morning. Now, under the hot sunshine of early afternoon, taking a picnic to the island felt like tackling an obstacle course. Lucy and Sam remembered their first expedition here. Scrambling over the stones had been difficult enough then, but at least they had been able to go on all fours whenever it had been too difficult to stay upright. This time baskets, bottles, rugs, flasks and bags all had to be carried over the rocky causeway. Many of the stones were round, sharp, or awkwardly angled. Some were unexpectedly unstable: 'rocky rocks', Sam called them, and they produced some hilarious moments.

"I'm not as young as I was," complained Dad, teetering dangerously with a picnic-basket at the end of one arm and a handful of air at the end of the other.

"He always says that when he's trying to get me to carry something for him," said Lucy, grabbing the basket. "The joke of it is, we do a lot of fell-walking in the Lake District and he never has this trouble on the stony paths there."

"Don't forget, Lucy," grumbled Dad, "when we go fell-walking in the Lake District we have our walking sticks; and fell-walkers have boots."

"Beach-walkers have bare feet," observed Sam, admiring Sue's easy passage over the causeway. She did not seem to grip the rocks with her toes or even stop to steady herself, but sprang from stone to stone as nimbly as a ballet-dancer.

"Go for the dry ones," she called back to them. "Anything wet is going to be slippery and you could really hurt yourselves in a fall here."

"We know," said Dad, just keeping his balance.....but he and the others arrived safely on the island, put down their picnic things, and could at last relax. Somehow, they felt it was right that they had had to struggle while Sue had skipped effortlessly on to the island. It was her island, and they were being granted privileged admission to her secret world. For a moment, as she stood alone in her miniature sea-swept garden where sea-pinks sprouted between the rocks and great blue vistas stretched before her, she was queen of her tiny country and they were her subjects, dropping gifts on the grass before her. It was surely impossible for anyone not to be in love with her, thought Lucy. Then Sue was smiling at them and spreading the rugs and had become once more their new, exciting, real friend--but there would always be an aura of splendour and mystery about her, thought Lucy: the lithe and sun-bronzed mermaid, the golden-curled goddess, the barefoot, stylishly-ragged, island queen.

Sue had recovered a huge umbrella from the storm-tossed debris of her house. Now they sat in its welcome shade to begin their meal.

"Is it a late lunch or an early tea?" enquired Sam, taking a cheese-and-onion sandwich.

"Doesn't matter," grinned Sue. "It's a picnic. You were right: your Dad makes a great picnic."

"You bring a great apple," answered Dad, choosing a green one.

"Good," said Sam. "I like the reds."

"I love this island," said Lucy, stretching out on the rug, keeping her head in the shade but letting the sun soak into the rest of her body. "I feel like a castaway."

"Castaways don't eat this well," said Sam, munching yet another cheese-and-onion sandwich.

"We were going to build a cairn here," Lucy continued, "on the first day we came over. But when we saw you we forgot all about it."

"We can still build one," said Sue. "In fact we should, all together."

"That's a lovely idea," said Lucy. "We'll each bring a stone from the causeway.....but later. I'm feeling lazy now after all that tea and cake."

"We'll need another shopping trip after this," Dad reminded them.

"The mobile shop arrives in the village tomorrow," said Sue. "I get my things there."

"That's handy," said Dad.

"Oh for goodness' sake," protested Lucy, "don't talk about shopping on a lovely afternoon like this. You'll be planning the housework next. I feel a million miles away from shops and I never want to have to go to another one."

"I know how you feel," laughed Sue. "You hate shops like I hate, well.....shoes."

"Yes, things of the town, and ordinary life, and work and money, and being grown-up and sensible," muttered Lucy. "I don't want to be sensible here."

"A very sensible young woman, then." Sue continued to laugh, but it was a kind laugh, not making fun of Lucy at all, who felt Sue understood her perfectly.

"You've got away from all that sort of thing by being here," Lucy went on. "I think you've been very clever. How did you manage it?"

"Lucy," Dad interrupted, "Sue may not want to talk about her private life, you know."

"I don't mind." Sue curled up into her 'mermaid' position near Dad. "I used to think I would mind, used to think I wanted to keep everything a secret; but now we're all friends I don't want to keep secrets--not from you, anyway."

"Tell us your secrets then," demanded Sam.

"Not all at once," laughed Sue.

"Now we've been rude." Lucy sat up, feeling embarrassed. "You're our lovely new friend and we're making you tell us things you don't have to tell us. We all apologise," she glared at Sam, "don't we?"

"I'll tell you why I came here." Sue rolled on to her front and picked a long sea-pink from a bunch growing beside her. She looked intently at the little flower. "I came here because I was very unhappy at home--which is a long way away--and needed to be on my own, somewhere beautiful and quiet where other people wouldn't make me do things I thought weren't right. I was very lucky to find my little house just when I needed it. Now I've been very lucky again: to find new friends just when I needed you."

She gave the flower to Lucy, who put it in her hair.

"My father wanted me to marry someone I didn't love." Sue found another sea-pink and turned it in her suntanned fingers. "I wouldn't marry anyone without love, true and proper love, but my father thought other things were more important. My father's very powerful, difficult to argue against. He's not a bad man, but I believed he was wrong about this, so I did have a very big argument with him and ran away at the end of it. That's not like me. I usually stay and fight--but I had no more fight left in me."

"But you fought in your own way to find your little house and this new way of life," said Lucy, full of admiration for the beautiful woman who had fought for true love.

"Yes, I suppose I did. That's why, when my house was destroyed in the storm, I felt really bad and.....well, you know what I mean. You saw me."

"But we've fixed it for you now," said Sam, wanting to cheer her up.

"Yes," she smiled, "and I'm very pleased you have. I got used to being on my own," she continued, "and liked it more and more; but just recently I've come to see that can be rather selfish. Frankly, I'm very glad I wasn't on my own when the storm happened. You made me realise that."

"Well, you see," Dad spoke with a smile in his voice, "the arrival of a wandering, motorcycling family--unruly kids, father needing a lecture in childcare--hasn't altogether been a bad thing."

"We're not unruly," Lucy protested. "Who says we're unruly?"

"He's teasing us all," laughed Sue, "which is indeed no bad thing." She rolled over and lay on her back, closing her eyes to the sun. "It's a very long time since I've been teased--nicely teased, I mean."

"Remind me to do it every so often," said Dad quietly.

"But love is what really matters, isn't it?" Lucy was serious again. "That's what you believe; that's what you fought for, isn't it?"

"Yes. Love and understanding and acceptance and respect."

"All those things *are* love," declared Lucy.

"Someone's going to be very lucky when they marry you," said Sue.

"Someone's going to be very lucky when they marry you," answered Lucy.

Sue looked away, out to sea.

"Will you promise me something?" asked Sam unexpectedly.

"Mmm?" Sue rolled over to face him.

"Will you teach us to swim under water--before you get married?"

"Tomorrow, if it's calm." Sue gave him a kind look which stopped Dad and Lucy laughing. "I promise not to get married for a long time."

"Don't wait too long." Lucy planted a kiss of friendship on her cheek. "Come on, Sam, we'll find the first stones for our cairn."

They went back to the causeway and started to choose stones small enough to carry but large enough to serve as building-blocks for the cairn.

"Shall we build it on the seaward side," asked Sam, "on top of the little cliff above the mermaid's rock?"

"Good idea," answered Lucy.

"Then sailors will see it," added Sam, "as well as people on the beach, and we'll always know it marks a special spot."

"Let's just collect the stones here for now," said Lucy. "We'll leave Dad and Sue on their own."

"Why?"

"You'd like her in the family, wouldn't you? I mean all the time, not just on holiday."

"Of course. She's great."

"Well, we'll start by leaving them together for a while."

"Will that really make her join the family?"

"It should help. Just wait and see. You think she's beautiful, don't you?"

"You bet I do!"

"Well, so does Dad."

"Does he? He hasn't said so."

"Believe me, Sam, he does. He's falling in love with her. He'll want to marry her, and then we'll have a new mother."

"Wow! Sue as our new mother. Beautiful and clever and special and strange and.....a mermaid. That'll be wonderful!"

"You've got the idea; now we just have to give her time to fall in love with him."

"Wait a minute, clever-clogs." Sam dropped an armful of stones on their heap. "She may not want to get married, to Dad or to anybody. You heard her talking about how she likes being on her own here--and anyway, she promised me not to get married for a long time."

"Grown-ups keep changing their minds, Sam."

"What'll we do then? Tell her we'll make a new family together? Tell her Dad will love her and be kind to her and that we'll always come on holiday here?"

"No, Sam. Whatever you do, please don't do that. We won't *tell* her anything. We'll just give her time to get to know us and show her how much we love her. She's been unhappy, she wants to be happy, and now she can be--with us. It's really very simple."

"Grown-ups are never very simple," said Sam, throwing another stone on the heap.

"Hey, you two!" It was Dad's voice. He and Sue were walking towards them. "How's the cairn coming along?"

Lucy looked at Sam.

"Remember now," she said.

"Remember what?" asked Dad.

"Er.....remember we want to build the cairn onthe other side of the island, overlooking the sea. We're just collecting good stones here."

"Right," said Sue. "We'll help you carry them across."

"We'll need lots more," said Sam.

"Mind you don't drop them on your toes," Dad warned Sue.

Steadily, they collected stones and built the cairn on top of the little cliff where Lucy and Sam had hidden to watch the mermaid on her rock.

"This is where we first saw you," explained Sam. "We're going to mark the spot for ever."

"My son is one of the last great Romantics," declared Dad.

"I hope there are a few more," said Lucy quietly.

"And talking of romantic ideas," continued Dad, "what's going to be 'the precious thing' you hide under the cairn?"

"I don't know," answered Lucy. "We'll have to think about that."

"I'll give you something," Sue's voice sounded soft and far away as she looked out to sea again, "if you can wait until tomorrow."

"All this waiting," moaned Sam, lifting two more stones. "It's harder than building a house and a cairn."

Chapter 12   Swimming with the Mermaid

After the picnic they left the island before an incoming tide returned to cover the causeway. Sue went back to her house. Dad--insisting he and the children would do the washing-up--led Lucy and Sam back to theirs. Tidying up took a long time. Lucy put herself in charge of making sure all their swimming costumes were ready for the next day, hoping the tide and weather would allow their adventure to continue-- and hoping for much more, hoping for things she could scarcely put into words.

"Shall we ask Sue to supper again?" Sam held up an extra plate.

"I think she'll want some time on her own after today," said Dad. "We mustn't take her over, you know."

"Don't you want to see her again, Dad?"

"Of course I do. But remember, she's a very private person with things to do in her own house--especially now she has to put it all in order again. We'll see her tomorrow if she says the water's safe for swimming."

It was a restless night. Lucy and Sam were tired after their long and exciting day, but they didn't feel like going to bed. They knew Dad was restless, too: not talking much, moving about and re-arranging things in his own room now Sam was back with Lucy. They stayed up to look at the stars: more and more appearing in the vast, luminous dome above the empty beach and calm water, diamond-white on ice-blue, awesome and magnificent. Beyond the faintly hissing sea they could just make out their newly built cairn on the far coast of the island, marking their special spot and seeming to anchor all the excitement and happiness they had found in this place--and some of the anxiety, too. Much closer, only a few yards away, they could see Sue's house with lights behind the window, and imagined her inside. They knew her now. They were friends with the mermaid, but they knew she was more than a friend and more than a legendary creature made real. She was an intriguing new person in their lives, able to bring wonder and happiness into their family.....if only she had really fallen in love with Dad and he had really fallen in love with her and everything worked out as it should. If only no-one spoiled it; if only no bad luck came to change it;

if only no worrying concerns of grown-ups--which they knew could complicate every decision--came to ruin their plans.

* * *

As always, everything looked better and seemed clearer with the Skylarks and sunrise. It was going to be another beautiful day with only a few happy-looking clouds along the horizon, a calm sea, and scarcely any wind. Surely this would be safe for swimming.....only Sam wondered how cold it would be.

"The North Sea," grinned Dad. "It'll be cold all right. We mustn't stay in too long."

"We'll come out on to the rocks and warm ourselves like seals," said Lucy.

"Then the hot sun will make the water seem even colder," said Sam. "We could smear ourselves with butter, like Channel swimmers."

"Not enough butter," said Dad, reserving it thankfully for his toast.

They did not have to wait long before Sue was seen leaving her house.

"She looks different," observed Sam.

"That's because she's wearing a dress," explained Lucy. "She dresses up for going in the sea, because the sea is so important to her. I like that."

"But the last time we saw her swimming, hadn't she taken her clothes *off*?"

"Well, perhaps the sea is so important to her that sometimes she wants nothing between her skin and the water. I like that, too. But today she'll have a swimsuit on under that dress. I hope it's the purple one."

They waved and shouted 'good morning' as Sue approached the house. She did look different in a sleeveless Summer dress with little flowers printed on the cotton and white buttons down the front. They also noticed a fine gold chain around her neck, which had previously been bare and unadorned.

"She's dressed for a party," whispered Sam.

"She looks lovely," breathed Lucy. "Next time I go to a party--I mean a Summer daytime party--I'm going to wear a dress like that, with no shoes and just one gold chain necklace."

"But you don't go to Summer daytime parties," objected Sam.

"But if I ever do," sighed Lucy.

"Hi there!" Sue came up to the front door. "I do think it's safe for swimming."

"Hooray!" cried Sam.

"I thought you would have your swimsuit on under that dress," smiled Lucy. "You look lovely."

"Thanks."

"Will it really be safe?" asked Dad, offering her a cup of tea.

"Should be. I'll check the currents before we go anywhere deep. We'll be all right just splashing about off the beach."

"What I really want to do is dive off your rock," admitted Sam.

"Perhaps later," said Sue. "Everybody ready?"

"Not quite," explained Lucy. "We weren't sure if we should put on our swimming things or not. Come on," she said to Sam, "let's get changed--and I've got to push all my hair under a bathing cap."

From their bedroom, Lucy and Sam could hear Dad and Sue talking quietly in the sunshine outside the front door.

"Lucy's right," Dad was telling her, "you do look lovely."

"Thank you. I'm not used to compliments here--or anywhere, frankly."

"You'll have to get used to them from us," Dad was saying. "The children are very impressed." There was a pause. "Do you really swim in that?" Was Dad being bold enough to touch her golden chain, her dress, or the purple swimsuit Lucy guessed would look so smart it really shouldn't get wet?

"Oh, my necklace? Yes, it's tight enough to stay on."

"Very stylish.....but out here, in this wild place, shouldn't it be a necklace of sea-shells?"

"I can only bear gold on my skin, and not too much of that."

"You see, the kids think you're a mermaid."

"I shall be--for them."

* * *

The water was very cold, even in the small-rippled shallows just off the beach where the golden-sanded sea-bed pulsated under refracted sunlight. They splashed about, Sue and Dad swimming easily a little farther out and seeming to become better and closer friends as they did so, Lucy and Sam doing breast-stroke and back-stroke towards the shore. They never became completely used to the cold, even after some time of quite energetic swimming, and--just as Sam had predicted--whenever they stood up into the hot sunshine, going back into the water was a chilly shock. Only Sue seemed fully relaxed in the sea, floating serenely on her back, doing aquabatic rolls and coming up with a nonchalant shake of her head and eyes wide open, as blue as the Summer sky.

"How do I stay under?" Sam called across the sun-sparkled wavelets. "I keep bobbing up!"

"That's because you're full of air," said Dad.

"But if I'm not full of air I'll drown!" He looked pleadingly at Sue. "You're going to teach me."

"Come out a little deeper," she said, gliding beside him. "You have to tuck your legs up and dive down forwards. Put your arms down like this."

She demonstrated a forward roll, her feet appearing briefly on the surface, then Sam could see her swimming a few strokes along the sandy bottom. She came up, shook her head, and gulped in new air.

"There now," she smiled. "Can you keep your eyes open under water?"

"Oh yes," said Sam. "It stings, but I don't mind."

"I'll go down and watch you," said Dad, his head dropping out of sight like the rounded stern of a sinking ship.

Sam tried the roll. He breathed in and tilted forwards, enveloped in a roaring silence as he thrashed about, trying to not to inhale, keeping his eyes open. He saw Dad and Sue completely submerged and waving at him--then he burst up again, gasping and spluttering.

"I didn't stay down very well," he complained.

"Use your hands like paddles to dig down through the water," explained Sue.

"Like the planes of a submarine," said Sam

"That's the idea."

"I knew there'd be some science in it."

Sam tried again, kicking his legs and turning his hands to ensure a downward thrust. Once more the cold blueness enveloped him, the sea-bed rolled like a pilot's horizon, the light filtered down in eerie pulsations to dance as if in tentacled life over mysterious rocks. Suddenly he could steer himself level, go deeper, pass that clump of waving seaweed--then he was bursting up again into hot and friendly sunshine.

"I'm getting it!" He sounded thrilled, but tired. "If only I could stay down longer."

"Not too much at once," smiled Sue.

"Can we swim round to your rock?" asked Lucy.

Sue looked at Dad.

"D'you think they could manage it?"

"I think so, if we hug the shore of the island on the way. It's not too far, is it?"

"No, but it's deep off there. Have a rest and I'll check the current."

Dad led Lucy and Sam back to the shore, wading up the sand once the water was at waist height, but Sue sped off in a powerful crawl, directly out to sea.

"Look at her go," said Sam, full of admiration, "and she's under water most of the time."

"That's the fast Australian crawl," explained Dad. "She'll be half-way to Australia before lunch."

"She's heading straight for Norway," said Sam.

"Now she's turning in behind our cairn." Lucy was watching for the re-appearance of Sue's head or the splash of her arms. "Yes-- she's in sight again, waving. It must be all right."

"She's coming back," announced Sam, "like a submarine on the surface."

In a few moments the white wake subsided around Sue as she stood up and walked towards them, water streaming down her arms, the purple swimsuit dark on her golden body, her lips wide in a smile.

"Don't you think she's like a goddess coming out of the sea?" breathed Lucy.

"Yes," said Dad, "just like in the old stories."

"But real," said Lucy.

"It's very calm today," Sue reported, "quite safe if we all stay together. Are you ready?"

They slid back into the chilly water, swimming slowly along the edge of the newly-submerged causeway towards the Southern coast of the island. Suddenly the water was deeper with no immediate sense of the bottom, and much colder. They seemed to be riding the ocean in the same magical way they had sensed when they had watched Sue from *Albatross*. This morning was much calmer with only the gentlest swell, but the almost musical rise and fall of the sea was still beneath them: exultant and soulful, mysterious and powerful. They felt they could swim like this all day, if only the golden-skinned mermaid would stay with them; stay close and loving, wild but tender, and never leave them for her lonely life in the dunes or her more complicated life in a distant town. If they could go on like this, thought Lucy and Sam, they could be completely happy. Now a little tired, they reached the corner of the island and could see the mermaid's rock and their small cairn above it on the cliff top. They struck out more strongly for the rock, were pleased to grasp its shell-encrusted bulk, and hauled themselves out of the water on to the tiny beach at the base of the cliff.

"The secret beach," exclaimed Dad. "It's wonderful!"

"The mermaid's rock," said Lucy, turning to Sue. "You must sit on it, just so Dad can see you as we first saw you.....please."

Sue did, curling her legs up on top of the rock, brushing water from her hair with her hand, looking silently out to sea.

"You'll have to bring the camera and take a photograph of her," said Sam to Dad, who was looking at Sue with a strange smile.

"No," said Lucy. "A photograph would spoil the magic. We must remember her just like this, remember her our own way."

"Let's dry off and warm up in the sun," said Sue, breaking the spell. "You've done really well," she added to Lucy and Sam. "Great swimmers."

"You needn't have been so worried about us that first time," Sam reminded her.

"It was just that I cared about you," replied Sue. "Still do."

"I'm glad you care about us," said Lucy.

They dried off surprisingly quickly in the sun. Dad found a very hot and sheltered place to sit. They talked about seals and boats and fish and crabs and lobsters, but didn't see any of these things; only a pair of Puffins flying quickly Northwards, low over the sea. It was magnificently lonely on this side of the island, and they all knew why Sue had come to love her secret place so much.

"Let's have one more swim," said Lucy.

"I want to see you dive in off that rock again," pleaded Sam.

Sue obliged with a neat back flip. She bobbed up and said she wouldn't do that again now the tide was falling. Sam jumped in off the rock; Lucy waded in.

"Before we head out there I'll just find you something for the cairn."

Sue's matter-of-fact words did not seem to go with the splendour of her smooth and curving plunge to the sea-bed. Lucy and Sam put their faces under and saw her 'walking' on her hands along the sandy, rock-strewn floor, very much in mermaid-style, sending up only a few bubbles, so perfectly could she control her breath. Then she was rocketing back to the surface and bursting up with a huge smile--and a small shell held aloft in her delicate fingers.

"You *knew* it was there!" squealed Sam.

"It's beautiful!" cried Lucy, swimming over to look. "It's not alive, is it?"

"Of course not. You don't think I would take a live creature from its home, do you? No--this is a special present for your cairn. There aren't many of these shells about; mostly mussels and limpets here."

The shell was far more beautiful than any mussel or limpet. It was curved and pointed and its creamy smoothness was undamaged.

"From my special place to your special place," said Sue quietly. "Dad can look after it while we have our swim." She glided rapidly to the shore, dropped the shell on the beach below Dad, and plunged back in to join Lucy and Sam who were holding on to the rock. "We're going for one more swim!" she called back to Dad.

"I'll watch you," he answered. "I'm nice and warm here now."

"We won't go too far," Sue assured him.

They swam off the rock. Again came the feeling of vastness and isolation, the swell of the deep that was like music, a mysterious song of open oceans. The children swam close to Sue, floating up to her bright eyes. They held hands in the sea, their legs treading water. Out here, their faces right on the sea's surface, Dad and the island seemed a long way off; the beach and the houses even further. There was only the sea and the sky and the amazing woman beside them. Then once more came the sense of music they couldn't really hear but knew was swilling through their souls as the sea was swilling round the island and the whole World. This was indeed Sue's place; but now also their place--and now was the time to speak.

"We love you," said Lucy.

"Yes we do," said Sam.

"Will you marry Dad and stay in our family?"

"Will you be our new mother and our real friend as well?"

"Will you?"

"Will you?"

They stopped asking such things when they saw Sue's face. It bore an expression they had never known before. She might have been surprised, angry, pleased, shocked, thrilled, insulted, overjoyed--or all these things at once. For an instant they thought she was going to shout or cry. She suddenly ducked her head under the water and came up again, blinking salt from her eyes. Was it to wash away tears she did not wish them to see? Was it to clear her mind? They couldn't tell.....and always the sea swilled under them, lifting them up gently, letting them fall, sublime and powerful, like their own emotions. At last Sue smiled at them; they felt her hands tighten on theirs under the water as they rode the gentle swell together.

"I've never had such things said to me," she told them honestly. "I've never known such good people."

"But you do really want to be with us, don't you?" Sam paddled close to her.

"We do love you, but you have to really want to marry Dad," said Lucy. "Really, really--and really want to be with us."

"I think," Sue spoke slowly, "for the first time in my life, I really do. But you must understand, your Dad will have to ask me first."

"He's very shy," said Lucy.

"I understand. I'm shy, too."

"I never thought you were shy," said Sam. "You don't look shy."

"That's always been one of my problems, young man," Sue gave him a serious look, "but obviously not one of yours. Now, we must go back to your Dad. We've been in the water a long time."

They swam back towards the island, the rock, the tiny beach, and Dad waving at them; their easy strokes giving no hint of what was rushing through the children's minds. They looked at each other with a mixture of anxiety and excitement.

"You mustn't say anything about this to Dad," Lucy warned Sam. "Nothing. Not yet, anyway."

Safely back from what had seemed like a deep-sea adventure, their return to land was a disappointment to Lucy and Sam. Dad did not ask Sue to marry him and Sue said nothing about being ready to be asked. The children made no mention of their emotional confessions to Sue, far out there in the dark blue water when their spirits had been lifted by the swell and Sue's hand-clasp: firm, warm, and delightfully human in that wild and empty sea, it had seemed to confirm all their hopes. Placing the shell in the middle of the cairn was a special moment. They stacked stones around it carefully so as not to break it or let anyone see it was there--but now, nobody was talking about anything special as they walked and paddled back to the beach, the tide having dropped to expose the causeway once more. Dad said they should all put some energy back by having lunch at the Ship Inn, insisting that since Sue had taken them swimming, he should take them eating. So they went to their separate houses, washed off the salt and sand as best they could, and put on dry clothes. They felt invigorated by emerging from so much cold water into the delightful warmth of a sunny afternoon. Sue appeared in her dress again, and Dad led them up the beach to the village.

After their meal--this time with pots of hot tea--Sue prepared to go home. The children pleaded with her to stay longer but she told them they should have time to enjoy their holiday their own way.

"But we enjoy it most with you," said Lucy.

"Me too--but I still have things to put right in that mess of a house. We'll meet again soon."

They did not expect her to be a 'kissy' person, even after what they had said to one another out there in the open sea, but she bent to kiss both Sam and Lucy on the cheeks. Then Dad stood up and took her hand and kissed her as well--but to Lucy's disappointment it was only on the cheek, and didn't look like the sort of kiss a man should give a woman when he was going to ask her to marry him. Then suddenly Sue wasn't there, leaving only a great emptiness.

"I miss her already," said Sam sadly.

"I'll always miss when she's not here," said Lucy miserably.

"She's good fun, isn't she?" smiled Dad, reaching for more tea.

"Yes," said Lucy vehemently, "and don't you forget it!"

* * *

Another calm blue night was settling over the tiny houses in the dunes before Lucy spoke to Dad about Sue again. This time it was to ask the question she couldn't keep inside her any longer.

"So, Dad--when are you going to marry Sue?"

"Am I going to marry Sue?" Dad looked surprised, but not very serious; not angry, disapproving, secretly excited, or anything that Lucy might have hoped for or even dreaded. She knew this was going to be difficult.

"We love her, Dad. We want her in the family--and she wants to be. She said so."

"Oh yes?" said Dad evenly. "And when was this?"

"When we were swimming."

"Oh I see. So my children have married me off to a strange woman while I wasn't looking. I knew I shouldn't have let you two out my sight with her."

"But she's not a strange woman," argued Sam, "she's Sue. She's our best friend and she wants to be yours, too."

"Being best friends is one thing, being married is something else.....and look at me, Sam. Look at me and tell me she's not strange."

"Yes, but she's strange in wonderful ways, isn't she? We know you love her really, and she loves you. We can tell."

"Now wait a minute! We've only known her a few days. In fact we hardly know her at all."

"People in love know straight away," said Lucy quietly. "We know she's right for us."

"Maybe--but you don't have to marry the woman!"

"That's your job, Dad. You'll have to ask her. She said so."

Dad's voice was rising higher and higher.

"What d'you mean she said so?"

"She knows you're shy, but she still expects you to be the one who proposes marriage. She's shy, too."

"There's nothing shy about her!"

"Yes there is: she won't ask you."

"I should hope not, my girl! Now be honest with me, have you been stirring all this up?"

Lucy and Sam looked at the floor.

"Do you realise you could have made a very embarrassing situation for us all? Here's a strange young woman on her own, we've become friends through a quirk of fate with that storm, she's been very nice to us in her own way, perhaps we've gone a bit far in talking about personal feelings and emotions--but that's a far as it goes. Now my own children are going to make every minute we have to be here excruciatingly embarrassing because you've given her the completely wrong idea."

"But it's not the wrong idea, Dad--and it's her idea too. Don't be angry. You should be pleased she loves us in return. I know she does, in her own way--and she needs us to love her."

"Well we don't need *her* to love *us*."

"I think we do. I think you do most of all."

Lucy thought she had really gone too far and that Dad was going to be very angry, but worse than any anger she might have had to face was Dad's slow speech as he sat down on a stool opposite his children.

"Now look. You must see it wouldn't be right to marry Sue, whatever I might feel about her."

"So you *do* feel something. You do, you do!"

"Never mind that. Just think now: she's single, we're a family. She's from some rich background, we're just ordinary. We live in a big city, she doesn't like being with people....."

"She likes being with us."

"Yes, but this is on holiday. This isn't everyday life, and what she might have enjoyed with us doesn't make her in love with me."

"But she really *is* in love--and we know you are. Why don't you admit it, Dad?"

"All that aside, don't you see it would be wrong to marry her and take her away from this place to live in London? It would be like taking a wild sea-bird and putting it in a cage."

"We could live in London in the Winter and live up here in the Summer, then everyone would be happy."

"Well, my dears, I'm not going to argue with you or have raised voices any more. You think you have all the answers to this--but really, you've made far too much out of what's happened. Let's stay friends with Sue if she wants that, and not embarrass her or make ourselves look sillier than we must look already."

"The silliest thing of all would be to lose her, Dad."

Dad's mood darkened and they knew they should go no further with him.

"Now I think we should all go to bed. We're very tired and we'll make a fresh start in the morning--perhaps go exploring that lake, eh Sam? You can take the binoculars for bird-watching. Let's go off to bed now. Goodnight. Goodnight."

He kissed them as usual and they said 'goodnight', but when they had rolled themselves on to their bunks they did not feel good. They turned their faces to the wooden walls with the knowledge that all the beauty and wonder of their moments in the sea with Sue could be shared and celebrated and spread into the reast of their lives--or be lost for ever.

"It would have been our chance to have a new mother as well," said Lucy to herself--but Sam had heard.

"Well, that's okay. I don't need a new mother. I just need Dad."

"But Dad needs someone new, Sam, not just us. He needs a new person to love and to love him."

"Are you crying, Lucy?"

"Go to sleep, Sam. I'll be better in the morning. We'll all be better in the morning."

"No we won't."

Chapter 13   The Runaway

It was very early and very bright and the Skylarks were up again--but this morning there was a wind and a bigger noise from the sea as waves broke heavily on the beach. Sam turned his back to them and ran through the dunes, the tall and sharp marram grass giving way to short turf. Sam didn't need his map; he knew he was on course for the lake. Once he was there, he could hide in the reeds and watch the birds. There might be frogs in the soggy edges of the lake. There might be swans swooping overhead and coming down to the water. There would only be beautiful things at the lake, exciting things, natural things; nothing made by people, nothing to hurt him, disappoint him, or make him cry.

* * *

"Do you mean to tell me he crept out of here while you were asleep and you don't know where he is?" Dad stood half-dressed in the doorway. "Well?"

"He must have gone before I woke up," Lucy explained again.

"Are you sure you had nothing to do with this?"

"Honestly, Dad, I have no idea where he is. I just know he was upset last night. We all were."

"We'll be more upset if he gets himself lost or hurt somewhere out there." Dad was fastening his shirt. "Come on." He stepped outside with Lucy, shouting "Sam!" a few times and taking the binoculars with him. "You don't think he's on that island, do you?"

"Yes, he might be." Lucy watched Dad scan the rocks. "He was happy there."

"I thought we were all happy here," muttered Dad, "and now something like this has to happen."

Lucy had never seen Dad so worried, nor felt so helpless herself.

"I wish I'd woken up in time," she confessed.

"So do I," grumbled Dad.

"He could be with Sue," ventured Lucy, unsure what might follow from the mention of her name.

"Yes," Dad lowered the binoculars, "I was afraid of that."

"I'll go if you don't want to."

"Oh, I want to," scowled Dad, closing the door with a bang to emphasise his mood. "I want to see her right away."

* * *

The lake lay in the middle of a grassy plain, the bottom of a wide bowl of dunes. The sea could not be heard; the sounds here were of rustling reeds, rippling water, and the calls of birds. As Sam approached he could hear the squawk of Black-Headed Gulls which must have bred here earlier in the Summer. Closer to the water's edge he became aware of the gentle gossipping of Mallard ducks, then the loud quacking of the drake as he squabbled with his mottled wives over a scrap of food. Crouching behind the reeds, Sam noticed a pair of swans gliding into view from behind a gull-covered island in the midle of the lake. The two adults, gleaming white in the morning sun, were leading four of last year's cygnets across the water. Sam knew the family was staying together in the way swans did--but he had had enough of families for the moment. He wanted some adventure on his own.

The first thing to do, he decided, was to circumnavigate the lake. The shore on which Sam was crouching was firm enough, but the Southern end of the lake looked as if it ended in a reedy marsh, and Sam guessed a small river must feed the lake from the North where the ground rose a little into the dunes. He would explore it and perhaps find its source; but first, the circumnavigation and a scouting of the marshes. He checked his watch and compass and set off.

There was an easy path on this side of the lake. Sam kept an eye on the central island which seemed to rotate as he marched, but the path soon veered off towards distant farmlands and Sam found that if he wished to keep going round the shore he would have to make his way through the reeds. There was a possibility of discovering a Mallard's or a Moorhen's nest, which might make the heavy going worthwhile; at the same time he didn't want to get his feet wet, sink in the mud, or lose any of his equipment in the water. This wouldn't have bothered Sue, he reflected. She went everywhere with bare feet, and Lucy had taken to copying her, as if she enjoyed feeling grass or mud or stone under her toes and would be quite pleased to abandon her shoes for ever. That might be all right for paddling about on a beach, reckoned Sam, but real explorers were careful to keep their feet dry and were properly happy in a good pair of boots like his own. He headed away from the shore and followed a drier route on the grass, but even this was eventually swallowed by the reeds. To make his way round the Southern end of the lake Sam had to leap from clump to clump of dry grass until he was beyond the marsh. Then he was making his way up the Western shore towards the small river which was indeed feeding the lake just as he had expected.

He followed the river upstream for a short distance and saw it wasn't a proper river at all: just a stream oozing out of soggy ground. He returned to the lake and sat down to watch the birds.

It was lonely here--and he wanted to feel lonely. There was only the sky above him and the lake below and no people anywhere in sight--and he did not want to see people. People were trouble. Even his own family was trouble. Dad would not marry Sue. Lucy was trying to make it happen but it wouldn't happen. Sue was beautiful and lovable, but Dad had been right when he'd said she was strange. Everyone was strange, thought Sam, if you looked at them long enough. He didn't want to look at anybody. He wanted to be on his own. On his own he would be all right; looking at the land and understanding what he saw. He loved the land and the land would be kind to him. He was a Bushman in the Kalahari, an Aborigine on the banks of the Murrumbidgee, an Iroquois brave in the woods of Delaware. He was an adventurer exploring their lands. He was also himself: map-maker of Albatross Bay. He knew his way around. He would be all right. Then there was a splash in the lake ahead of him. He looked down to see a Moorhen with her late brood of chicks: five balls of black fluff bobbing on the water behind her with those distinctive red tufts on their tiny heads. Here was another little family, all together, depending on one another, safe in their home with a mother to look after them. Then Sam did not feel so happy, sitting alone under the empty sky.

* * *

"I have not seen your son today." Sue looked very serious, hastily tying a blouse above the waist of her jeans. "He has not been here. I don't know where he is any more than you do." She ended her declaration with a blue-eyed stare directly into Dad's face. "I've had nothing to do with his disappearance."

"We can discuss that later," replied Dad, obviously unconvinced. "Sam was upset, I know that much. It's not like him to run away. I want to know what he's run away from. Is it you?"

"No." Sue slammed her door behind her. "It is not me. Your children have made it quite clear they want me to spend more time with them; they would never want to run away from me." Her eyes stared again. "Could it be you?"

"Why would Sam want to run away from his own father?"

"That's a matter for your conscience. Perhaps you've frightened him, disappointed him, or put unfair pressure on him."

"Are you daring to tell me how to look after my children again?"

"Yes!"

There was a furious silence--which Lucy had to break.

"Will you two stop arguing and start looking?"

They both looked at her.

"Not at *me*, you idiots! I think he'll have gone to the island and he might be hiding on the far shore below our cairn."

"That's the most sensible thing I've heard so far this morning." Sue brushed past them heading straight down to the beach. "Are you coming? The tide's rising already."

As soon as they found themselves on the level sand, Sue stopped them.

"Better idea," she snapped. "You scout through the dunes. If *Albatross* is still beached, he's not out rowing. Try down at the village; he may be looking at the boats there. I'll get out over the rocks faster than you can. If he's not on the island I'll come straight back and we'll head down the other end towards the castle. Okay? Let's go."

Dad did not go.

"Before we do any of that.....I want to apologise....for being too hasty.....for being sharp with you. I was just worried. You really do care about my children, don't you?"

Lucy saw them look at each other with new tenderness.

"Yes I do, more than time allows me to say right now."

Despite what she had said, they seemed held by each other's eyes.

"You really are a remarkable person," said Dad, his angry expression fading into a smile.

'Not now', thought Lucy. When she had wanted Dad to fall in love he hadn't bothered and now he was paying Sue compliments when there wasn't the time. It was maddening!

"Come on," Lucy pulled him away, "let's get going!"

Chapter 14   The Return of the Poet

The sun rose higher, the air grew hotter. Sam recognised a change in the atmosphere. The open blue sky began to fill with small clouds as the stillness of dawn gave way to a light breeze and new stirrings in the grass. He recognised another feeling too: hunger. He had come out with no breakfast: not a good idea for any explorer. He could also hear distant but faintly disturbing shouts, which he guessed were made by a family coming to play and picnic on the beach. Flutterings from the reeds suggested Mallards taking off. They would be in search of breakfast, thought Sam. He still felt lonely, but no longer quite alone. In this new mood he left his reedy hiding place and continued his walk around the lake--and was not surprised to see another human figure striding towards him. He was surprised, however, to recognise it as the poet.

"Hello there!" The poet waved as he came up to Sam. "You don't look too happy, young fella. You're out very early all by yourself."

"I like to be out early," Sam did his best to explain. "I came to explore the lake and watch the birds. I was just walking round to look at the hide here."

"Mmm." The poet shoved his hands in his pockets with a look suggesting he knew there was more to Sam's story than this. "Well now. I'm back early, too--much earlier than I expected. Shall we have a look in the hide together?"

The hide was a tiny hut, very close to the water's edge. Its planks were covered with moss and its roof with grass. Bending inside and closing the door behind them, Sam and the poet opened a panel in the lakeside wall and were granted a close-up view of the birds on the water and the miniature island directly ahead of them.

"Like gunners in a tank," exclaimed Sam, intrigued with the secretive position.

"Definitely no shooting allowed here," replied the poet, "except with a camera. You didn't bring your binoculars."

"I left in a hurry," shrugged Sam.

"Mmm," said the poet.

They looked at the birds for a while.

"There can be Gldeneye and Wigeon here, and Coots and Moorhens, even geese," explained the poet, " but this morning we only have the gulls and the swans."

"And that pair of Mallards," observed Sam before they fell silent again.

At last he felt he had to tell the truth, or at least more of the truth. He liked the poet and felt safe in his quiet but gently exciting company.

"Thanks for letting us row in *Albatross*," said Sam.

"That's all right," smiled the poet.

"I didn't just come bird-watching," confessed Sam. "I ran away."

"Was that a good idea?"

The poet wasn't particularly surprised or angry or ready to scold him. That made Sam feel better.

"Don't know," said Sam. "I was angry with my dad for not wanting to marry Sue, and I was angry with my sister for being bossy and trying to organise everything." He was running out of confession. "I was just angry," he stated finally, wondering what the poet would say.

"You need to be on your own sometimes, don't you?"

"Yes," said Sam.

"Me too." The poet kept looking out at the birds. "Does your dad really want to marry Sue?"

"Well," Sam did his best to explain, "he said it wouldn't be right; but Lucy and me, we know it would be right. We could have a mum again. I said I didn't care about having a new mum and I ran away, but I do care really. I'd like a new mum, especially Sue. We love her and want her in the family and we know she loves us and Dad as well; and we can tell Dad loves her, deep down he does. He's just shy and silly about it."

"Lots of men are shy and silly about being in love," said the poet.

"I know. People never think I'm old enough to understand these things--but I do understand."

"Of course," smiled the poet. "We also have to understand that people might be in love but wouldn't be happy if they got married; there might be all kinds of differences between them which would make a family life difficult. It's hard to think like that when you find someone very beautiful who enjoys being with you, but I suspect your dad is thinking like that. It's very sensible of him, but we shouldn't be sensible *all* the time. Do you think your dad *really* loves Sue?"

"Yes."

"If he really does, he must say so and not lose her if she honestly wants to be with him and with you children. It's a wonderful thing to have happened to all of you and the opportunity shouldn't be wasted."

"That's what Lucy says--or something like that."

"Lucy is right."

"How do you know all this?"

The poet folded his arms along the ledge of the hide's window, rested his head on them, and looked out over the lake.

"I know because I *did* waste the opportunity."

"What," exclaimed Sam, "were you in love with Sue as well?"

"No," the poet chuckled, "not Sue. I like Sue and think she's fun, and she's beautiful, too, isn't she? But I wasn't in love with Sue. This was someone else, many years ago; oddly enough, here, in this same place. I found her here, like treasure on the beach, but I did not hold her well enough, tenderly enough, honestly enough. So I lost her, and it was my own fault--and this must not happen to your dad." There was a pause, then he added quietly: "O for a Muse of fire."

"What's that?" Sam looked puzzled.

"Henry the Fifth: you've heard of him, the English king with the best speechwriter in history--and the worst haircut."

"The battle of Agincourt," said Sam proudly.

"That's the fella."

"But what is a Muse of fire, and why d'you want one?"

"Well," explained the poet, "at the start of Shakespeare's play about Henry the Fifth, an actor asks for a Muse of fire to help him describe the horses and the armies and all the excitement of the battle. So, a Muse of fire would be someone to help me find the right words to express what has to be said here. We're talking about some of the most important things in people's lives--you know that, and I know that--but it's easy to miss the best words, or say the wrong ones. It's supposed to be my job to find the best ones, then put them in the best order. Poets, you know; that's what we're supposed to do."

"I think you've used the right words," said Sam. "I understand what you mean about Dad having to speak out if he loves Sue. He mustn't lose the treasure *he* found on the beach. You lost your treasure on the beach, and that's why you come back here trying to find her, isn't it?"

Sam saw a strange smile turned upon him.

"You, my lad, are in danger of becoming a poet."

"I want to go home now," said Sam.

"Good idea," said the poet, and they left the hide together.

* * *

"Nothing." Sue was breathlessly back from her scramble over the causeway and her run up the beach. "He's not on the island and he's not swimming off the rocks and he's not....." she panted, ".....anywhere.....under water.....thankfully....."

Lucy and Dad saw her clothes were soaking wet and her hair still sparkled with water running down her neck.

"You swam round to look for him?"

"Yes," she gasped, pressing water out of her jeans, "I couldn't come back without checking properly; nothing to it, really."

"I don't agree," said Dad, full of admiration. "You're incredible. I don't know how to thank you for all your help."

"Haven't been much help yet," Sue gulped.

"Yes you have," replied Dad calmly. "The rowing-boat's still there; no sign of him in the dunes around the house. Lucy checked the harbour end of the beach."

"Nothing," reported Lucy.

"Right," Sue took charge once more, "we'll try the lake."

"The lake?"

"Sam's interested in bird-watching, isn't he?"

They nodded.

"The lake, then. This way."

* * *

".....not just battles, or people murdering kings, or stabbing Romans, or chopping each other's heads off, or ghost stories, oh no," the poet was telling Sam, "Shakespeare knew how to write about people being in love as well. He knew how important it is....."

"Oh no," groaned Sam, sitting himself down petulantly on the sandy grass as three figures appeared over the next dune. "Now I'm really going to be in trouble."

"You'll be all right," the poet assured him. "Just tell the truth."

The next few moments were full of waving and shouting and angry glances and raised voices and even some of those swear-words

Dad had learned in the Navy. Then there were apologies and explanations and tears and admissions and thanks and promises and cuddles and kisses.....and there was Dad kissing Sue as if he had never been shy at all.

"Did you really mean to run away?" asked Lucy when some of the confusion had died down.

"Yes," Sam answered, remembering the poet's advice to tell the truth, "but not very far, and not for very long."

Dismissing Dad's thanks with "it was nothing at all, we just met up at the lake for a chat", the poet went back to his house saying he had to leave again immediately, anyway. Sue returned to her house. Dad opened the door of their own cottage.

"You stay here," he said, "and I mean stay!" He looked at Sam as if he had been a naughty spaniel.

"He's going to help Sue get dry," explained Lucy as soon as Dad had gone. "She swam around the island looking for you, you know; even under water, in case you'd drowned. That's how much she cares about us. She led the search party. Of course we didn't know you'd already been rescued by the poet. Dad's very impressed with everything Sue did this morning. You should be, too. You caused a lot of fuss, but I think it just might have the happy ending we want."

"Sue's never needed any help getting dry before," observed Sam suspiciously as he looked out of the window.

"Things could be different from now on, Sam. We just need to leave them together for a while."

"Oh I get it," smiled Sam. "You mean when they come out of there they'll be married."

"More like.....sort of.....engaged."

Chapter 15   The Goddess from the Sea

Lucy and Sam made their own lunch. The cottage seemed lonely with Dad away at Sue's.

"Don't look so miserable, Sam." Lucy grinned at him over the dishes. "We wanted them to get together. Now they have, we should be pleased."

"It just feels funny," said Sam, crumbling his last biscuit. "I know Dad's only a few yards over there, but he seems miles away now."

"I know--but think how he must have felt this morning when you couldn't be found anywhere: much worse. We know exactly where Dad is. Cheer up. You didn't get into too much trouble for running away, and we'll all feel a lot better soon, believe me. Look," she pointed out of the window and stood up, "here they come now!"

The door opened. Dad and Sue were holding hands, which made each of them look different. Suddenly, everyone was smiling big smiles.

"Well," announced Dad, "I was wrong about thinking I shouldn't marry Sue. I should have married her years ago.....and if I'd known her, I would have. And I'll tell you something else: I've never been so pleased to be wrong about anything in my life."

"I was wrong, too," smiled Sue, "I mean at first, about your Dad. I thought he was less than the wonderful man he is."

"So," Dad closed the door, "you could say the old proverb isn't true: two wrongs *do* make a right--as long as you know you were wrong in the first place."

In the middle of their new happiness, everyone began to look puzzled. Sue ended the verbal confusion with a laugh.

"Really," she giggled, "this is too much. Let's just say we've got it right at last."

"We are going to be married," Dad confirmed at last, "but....."

Lucy felt she would explode if he introduced another problem.

".....we thought," Sue took up the explanation, "well, we thought we would ask you first, just to make sure you're really happy about it."

Dad gave a horrified look into the silence that had fallen across the room.

"You do think it's a good idea, don't you?"

"Yes! Yes! Yes!" screamed Lucy and Sam.

"Absolutely sure?"

That was Sue, somewhere in the middle of the yells, hanging on to Dad's hand.

"Yes! Yes! Yes!"

"That'll be a 'yes', then," said Dad when the shouting had stopped.

The children kissed him, then they kissed Sue, then they were kissed by Sue and Dad. Indeed there was more hugging and kissing in that little wooden room than Lucy, Sam, Dad, or Sue had known before.....which semed very good evidence that they had made the right decision.

"We need a party," decided Lucy.

"This is a party," grinned Dad, still being hugged.

"A big picnic with drinks and a bonfire," suggested Sam, hopefully.

"Every girl wants an engagement party," stated Lucy.

"Even me," smiled Sue into Dad's face.

"What about tonight?" urged Sam. "A party on Sue's island."

"With drinks and a bonfire," winked Dad.

"Yes! Yes!"

"I'll even order a special low tide," said Sue, glancing out of the window at the causeway.

"I'll go to the farm for bacon and eggs," said Dad.

"A barbecue!" shouted Sam.

"And I'll bring my last bottle of brandy," added Sue, "my *only* bottle of brandy, in fact."

"Brandy?" Sam's eyes popped. "Sailors and explorers should drink rum, but I suppose brandy will do."

"Just a taste," said Dad, "just this once."

"You will wear your pretty dress, won't you?" pleaded Lucy. "And the gold chain; and put flowers in your hair like a real mermaid would....."

"Seaweed," corrected Sam, "and her hair's too short anyway."

".....because this is a really special party, our best party ever."

"I'll do what I can," promised Sue.

"What'll you do for an engagement ring, Dad?" asked Lucy-- and Sue looked quizzically at him.

"I'll.....er.....I'll think of something."

"I see," smiled Sue. "This is going to be some party. I really *should* dress up."

"Nothing too formal, Darling," quipped Dad, "not in front of the puffins."

"Best beachcomber gear, then. I'll find some outfit."

"Promise you won't spoil it by wearing shoes," requested Lucy, pushing off her own sandals and feeling the floor with her toes.

"Don't worry." Sue patted Lucy's head gently. "This bride goes barefoot."

* * *

The afternoon was spent busily between the two houses. Lucy and Sam put themselves in charge of organising the party while Dad went off to the farm for the promised bacon and eggs. Sue spent intriguingly long periods in her bedroom. Every so often she would come out to help pack a basket or chat to the children.

"An engagement picnic," she beamed. "I'll bet your Dad never expected this when he heard me telling him off in that boat. To be honest, I never expected it myself."

"None of us expected it," said Lucy, "not at first, anyway--but we're very glad it's happened. We can't tell you how pleased we are."

"Oh, you're telling me all right," answered Sue, "just by being happy."

"Is it going to be like this all the time when you and Dad are married?" asked Sam. "I mean fun, like this?"

"Well," replied Sue, "it should be fun of one kind or another. You'll be glad to know your good idea has been taken up: we'll spend the Winters in London and the Summers up here."

"Great! So you won't lose your little house and we won't lose our holidays."

"No. We'll just have to make them bigger: the house and the holidays."

She disappeared again with another mysterious smile.

"What does she keep doing in there?" asked Sam.

"Getting ready, I think," said Lucy. "Remember, she has to be a married woman from now on. A married woman has big responsibilities, especially if she's married to our dad. She has to be our new mum as well. She's just, well, thinking, I suppose. Perhaps she wants time on her own, wondering if she'll be good at it."

"I think she'll make a brilliant married woman, and she's not even married yet. It's a good thing she said 'yes'--but we wouldn't have lost her even if she'd said 'no'."

"What d'you mean?"

"If Dad couldn't have married her I'd have married her myself."

"Really, Sam. It'll be a relief when you grow up." Lucy thumped a big bottle of lemonade into a basket, then found herself smiling. "On the other hand," she muttered, "it'll be a great loss."

Dad returned laden with food. He had bought bacon and eggs and milk and bread and sausages at the farm, then walked to the inn and bought a bottle of white wine.

"It should have been Champagne, of course," he admitted, "but they didn't have any. They weren't even supposed to sell me this but I told them it was for something really special. They let me have these glasses, too." He held up a pair of very elegant wineglasses. "Don't worry," he smiled, "I brought four, so we can all drink to our new life."

Lucy gave him a kiss.

"I always knew you were the best Dad in the world."

"Let's hope Sue thinks as well of me."

"Oh, that'll be no problem," chirped Lucy. "You only have to be her husband. It's much tougher being our dad."

* * *

The tide had fallen, the sea hissed softly upon the empty beach, and gulls' wings were tinted gold as late afternoon sunshine streamed form the Western sky. Below their blue vault, mountains of cloud were ranged along the sea's horizon, their bulbous tops already a delicious pink, as if an entrancing fairyland might lie beyond their peaks, or Paradise be reachable between their soft-walled valleys. Sam was watching Fulmars on their effortless glide along the dunes; Lucy was tying back her newly-washed hair with a blue scarf when a gentle knocking was heard at the door.

"That'll be your fiancée," she smiled.

When Dad opened the door and blue and golden light flooded in, they saw a tall figure silhouetted against the sea and sky. The figure was blue and golden, too: blue in the long gown draped dramatically down Sue's body; golden in the gleam of her short hair catching the sunlight, the glint of her thin necklace, and the sun-coloured skin of her arms and ankles. The gown was fastened elegantly on one shoulder leaving the other bare, and that too was golden, with sea light flaring behind the curve of her neck, gleaming around her throat and between her fingers. She seemed suspended in the light, somewhere between the sky and the door, the sun and the grass, the sea and their awestruck upturned faces. In a moment of stillness she shimmered before them, and they could only stare.

"The goddess from the sea," breathed Sam.

"Home-made!" Sue's dark laugh broke the spell--but nothing could diminish the glamour of her new appearance. "Do you like it?" she asked Lucy, holding out the skirt of her long gown.

"It's wonderful! A goddess's evening gown.....and you've remembered: mermaids *don't* wear shoes!"

"Nor, I see, do beach girls," smiled Sue, pointing at Lucy's bare toes with her own.

"You look delicious."

That wasn't a word Lucy and Sam had expected Dad to use, but they had to agree with him. Sue took their compliments with a very un-goddess-like shrug.

"Amazing what you can do with a bed sheet, a pair of scissors, and a party deadline."

"It is wonderful," said Dad.

"It's the woman inside the dress that matters," declared Sam. "I love your golden skin, it's gorgeous."

"He has a long and dangerous career as a charmer ahead of him," remarked Dad drily, "but he's right," he added, placing a kiss on Sue's bare shoulder.

"Come on, then," she ordered. "Party time on my island."

There was a scramble for picnic baskets, bags, and rugs--but Lucy and Sam stopped it with a quick look at each other and folded their arms in front of Dad and Sue.

"Oh no," said Lucy, "it's your engagement party, our picnic. You go on ahead together as honoured guests; we carry everything as honoured.....well, carriers."

"Imagine we're exotic porters attending the goddess's engagement feast," declared Sam, not quite balancing a box on his head.

There was going to be some grown-up reason for not doing this from Dad, and a grown-up maternal smile from Sue--but Lucy stopped them both.

"Go on--we'll bring everything!"

Dad glanced at Sue, Sue hoisted her gown to her knees, and they set off at a run together down the dunes and on to the beach.

"Look at them," muttered Lucy. "Like a pair of teenagers."

"I'll be a teenager soon," said Sam, struggling with three bags.

"Well I hope you have that much fun," said Lucy, watching the lovers take each other's hands as they reached the causeway.

When they had all clambered on to the island--Dad and Sue insisting they should help with carry   ing the large baskets over the rocks--they found their picnic spot in front of the cairn. Sam assembled the portable stove and lit its metal ring of methylated spirit. Luckily, there was scarcely any wind on this Summer evening, and when Sam pumped up the stream of paraffin it ignited at once and flared perfectly around the cast iron burner. Everyone was impressed by Sam's expertise. The roaring blue flame attracted all eyes as if its bright heat, both homely and exciting, would be the symbolic centre of their new life.

"Tonight I join the best family I could ever imagine," said Sue, somewhat unexpectedly putting their thoughts into words.

"Tonight we're a whole *new* family." Lucy's voice was affected by pride, delight, happiness, and all kinds of emotions she couldn't name easily. She thought she would say no more, but kiss Sue instead. Sue didn't look cuddly. Even kneeling at the stove she looked tall and stately in her magnificent rag of a gown. With her gleaming bare shoulder, her severely short hair and her suntanned, muscular arms, she looked indeed a goddess from the sea; but Lucy did cuddle Sue and kissed her on both cheeks. "I want you to understand how happy we are."

"I understand," replied Sue quietly. "You're a very special and lovable young woman."

The furious sizzling of bacon changed their mood as Dad did the cooking and everyone else held their plates. Soon there was a real barbecue picnic in progress, with much rolling-up of bacon, sharing of bread, balancing of fried eggs on buns, and eating with fingers; while crusts and scraps and pieces of bacon rind were tossed into the sea, attracting a few Black-Headed Gulls and even diverting the stately glide of the Fulmars. A yacht appeared off the Southern end of the bay, completing the seaside scene with a perfection of tall white sails rounding the castle point.

"She looks a beauty," remarked Dad. "Not much wind, so she's under full canvas; always looks good."

"Feeding time in Albatross Bay," declared Sam, throwing more bread to the gulls.....and it was.

"A toast!" Dad commanded, pouring out the white wine. "Didn't have any Champagne at the inn," he told them again, looking at Sue apologetically.

"This will be better," smiled Sue. "We'll always remember this wine."

They each raised a glass; a small one for Sam.

"To the new family," said Sue, before Dad could state whatever his toast was to have been.

"To the new family," they all said, and drank the wine, Sam's all at once.

"Since this is an engagement party," Dad put his glass down and turned to face Sue, "I must ask you to accept my ring--if it's still in one piece."

They all stared as Dad poked his fingers into his shirt pocket and drew out a small object. They all looked surprised. They had never seen a black engagement ring; it was a few moments before they realised the tiny circle was made of hair woven together in a strange twist. A few loose hairs made it a less-than-perfect circle, but that only gave it more honesty, romance, and wonder.

"It's my hair," explained Dad with an almost apologetic grin. "There'll be a proper ring later, of course."

"This is a proper ring; the best there could ever be." Sue's voice was quiet with emotion, and the children thought they could see the glint of tears in her smiling eyes.

"It's brilliant," said Sam. "Lucky you're not a bald dad, like Uncle Frank."

They all laughed.

"It....is.....quite.....wonderful," said Sue as Dad slowly placed the ring of hair on her finger. "It fits, too!"

They all laughed again--this time with a sense of relief.

"It was a difficult job, I can tell you: short notice, no special tools, not sure of the size, wiry and untameable hair."

"A labour of love," said Lucy.

"I learned about these in the Navy," Dad went on.

"Sailors can make anything," Sam interrupted.

"Yes, but this is actually a gypsy tradition: love token of the Romanies." Dad looked appealingly at Sue. "It should really have some of your hair in it, too."

"I don't have any to spare!" she laughed, rubbing her tiny curls.

"So it's just mine, I'm afraid. I thought: you don't have to be a true Romany to borrow a fine Romany tradition, as long as it's done sincerely."

"I accept," declared Sue.

"Thank you," said Dad with huge relief.

"This calls for a brandy," Sue got to her feet and rummaged in a bag, "even a tiny one for Sam."

"Not just yet," said Lucy, scrambling down to the water's edge. "Come on, Sam."

"Where are they off to?" asked Dad.

"I'm never going to forget this day," they heard Sue whisper.

"I should hope not," they heard Dad's chuckled reply, followed by the sound of a kiss.

In a few moments Lucy and Sam were back; Sam carrying a length of seaweed, Lucy a handful of long grasses and some sea-pinks. They flopped on to the turf at Sue's feet.

"I'm going to make you a mermaid's necklace," said Sam.

"And I'm going to make you a goddess's crown," said Lucy.

"See?" said Dad, reclining with a brandy glass in his hand and Sue's head against his chest. "We can make anything: spikey, wet, prickly, uncomfortable. The tortures are endless."

"Be quiet, Dad, and drink your brandy," ordered Lucy, "and drink Sam's too. It's not good for him."

"It shouldn't do a hardened sailor and explorer like Sam any harm to have one shot of spirits," said Sue from the comfortable recesses of Dad's arms.

"I've had a sip already and it's horrible," confessed Sam.

"Okay," said Dad.

"So I'll stick to the wine, thanks," added Sam, engrossed in his seaweed knotting.

"Isn't there an old legend that says once you've kissed a mermaid you can never go back to the land?" Lucy twined the grasses around her carefully-selected sea-pink blooms.

"Something like that," said Dad. "Anyway, I have kissed her and I don't want to go back."

"None of us ever do," said Lucy dreamily, "not now."

"I think the legend says you can go back," Sue's voice sounded soft and far away, "but if you do you'll never be happy, and you'll spend your whole life searching for the mermaid, trying to find her again."

"I've found her and I'm holding on to her," said Dad.

"And the mermaid will be unhappy for ever, too--if she is deserted by the man."

"She will never be deserted."

Sue seemed to sleep against Dad's chest, the Fulmars glided past along the small cliff of the island, the yacht gleamed white as it sailed closer to the shore, the sea hissed gently around the mermaid's rock, and the clouds along the horizon turned a luscious pink. At last the gifts were ready. Sue knelt on the grass in the middle of her island and Sam strung the seaweed around her neck. It lay against her golden skin looking wild and romantic. Sam kissed her cheek and backed away while Lucy placed the crown of grasses around Sue's brow. That too looked strange and beautiful, with the sweet sea-pinks against the short yellow curls. Lucy kissed Sue and stood back. Here was their glamourous and exciting friend who would be Dad's new wife and their own new mother; but here also--glimpsed suddenly in the middle of a silent sea--was the mysterious woman, mermaid and sea-goddess, enchanting and beautiful, wild and tender, remote, awesome, and thrilling. They saw her rise from her knees, stride to the edge of the island, place her naked feet on the cliff-edge rock, and raise her long arms into the blue air. What little breeze there was made tiny ruffles in her gown. Evening sunshine glimmered off the seaweed necklace and lit the flowers of her crown. She seemed held in magical light between sky and sea, between this moment and eternity. They were transfixed by her beauty, thrilled by her wonder. Then she dropped her arms to her sides, and the proud stance of a goddess was changed to the lonely figure of a woman looking out to sea. She turned to them with the strangest expression they had ever seen.

"I know that yacht," she sighed. "It belongs to my father."

She stepped down past the cairn and brushed her way through the tiny encampment that had been their picnic place. Dad caught her by the wrist.

"Don't be angry with me," she pleaded. "Leave me to sort this out."

"I'm not angry with you," Dad changed his hold to a tender cradling of her hands, "and I won't leave you. I'll marry you."

Chapter 16   A Millionaire drops Anchor

She came into the anchorage under bare poles, sliding slowly on a quiet engine: a yacht bigger and more splendid than any they had seen. Her gleaming white hull and superstructure were enlivened with glossily-varnished teak and brilliantly-polished brass. Her two masts soared up into the evening sky where coloured pennants fluttered above her ropes and wires. The massive booms with their furled sails seemed to run the length of her deck and led the eye back to a large Red Ensign flapping lazily at her stern.

In the stainless steel-railed pulpit on her bow stood the bulky figure of a man. His shirt and trousers were as white as his yacht. His suntanned head was bald and his face was trimmed with a dark golden beard. His feet--in immaculate deck shoes--were planted firmly on either side of the yacht's prow and beneath them her name could be read in golden letters: *Lady Susannah*.

"D'you think the yacht is named after Sue?" asked Sam.

Dad lowered his binoculars and gave them to Sam. Lucy did not like the expression revealed on his face.

"What does this mean, Dad? Why has Sue gone to her own house? What did you say to her in there when she'd rushed back off the island? Why can't we all be together like we should be?"

"We will be," Dad tried to sound confident. "Sue's just working some things out in her own place--but you should know she doesn't like her father interfering in her life. He once tried to make her marry someone she didn't love."

The words cut deeply into Lucy's already anxious mind.

"Yes, I remember her telling you; but that's all over, isn't it?"

Dad gave her a hard look.

"He's still a threat to everything she has here. You remember how precious her home is to her, how upset she was when the storm destroyed it."

"Yes," said Sam, "but we fixed it all up again for her."

"So we did--and we've fixed up a whole new life for her, haven't we? But her father may not approve of it. He may hate the idea of his daughter being married to a strange man with two children."

Lucy and Sam clamoured round Dad.

"You won't let him spoil everything, will you? He can't! He mustn't! Sue's engaged to be married. She's going to join our family.

We all love her and she loves us. It's all arranged. It's what she wants. He can't change that--can he?"

"Well," Dad put his arms round both his children, "Sue's going to talk to him now, and we must let her do this her own way. Look-- there she goes."

From their vantage-point at the front door they saw Sue emerge from her own house and run down the beach. She had stripped off the glorious blue gown and was wearing her purple swimsuit. It looked almost black between the darkening sea and the sky. In the stillness of the evening they heard the rattle of the yacht's anchor chain and its heavy splash into the water. A few moments later came the sound of Sue's dive into the sea and the steady strokes of her powerful crawl.

"We might have known she'd swim out rather than wait for a boat." Dad looked impressed. "That's my proud and independent girl," he added to himself.

"Of course," said Sam, as full of admiration as he was of anxiety.

Lights sprang up on the yacht as they watched the lithe body cutting luminous water. They remembered Sue on land, her skin warm and golden, her gleaming arms close to them--as now they seemed far away, ploughing through cold seas to take her even further from the brief but momentous happiness they had shared. The bulky figure of her father could now be seen at the stern, ready to help her aboard. Then there was nothing but the twinkling lights reflected on dark water, and the first stars gleaming innocent and pure far above the troubles of the World.

"Let's go in," said Dad flatly. "There's nothing we can do."

"We can be together and talk," said Lucy, lighting oil lamps and bringing a sense of family purpose back into their little room.

"Yes, that's very sensible," said Dad as they sat down at the table for coffee and biscuits. Lucy and Sam listened while Dad explained.

"Sue told me her father is very rich, probably a millionaire several times over."

"Wow!" grinned Sam, but Lucy didn't look pleased.

"He made his money in a business supplying food to big shops."

"That'll be why he's so fat," observed Sam, but Lucy didn't smile.

"He's never thought much of Sue's life up here; living in a shack, he calls it. He doesn't approve of what she does, what she wears, what she thinks. He even hates the idea of her swimming every day; apparently he can't swim and thinks it's dangerous and unhealthy."

"And just to annoy him, he's got a mermaid for a daughter," put in Lucy.

"Well," continued Dad, "you could say that. Everything Sue is seems to annoy him. Now he's come to try and persuade her to give up this way of life. Her mother's dead, there's no-one else in the family; when her father dies she could inherit all the money and live like a queen--but unless she changes her ways and lives what her father considers to be a normal life, he'll leave his entire fortune to his factory workers instead. You might call him a mad millionaire," concluded Dad with one of his faint smiles, "unless you're one of his factory workers, of course."

"But none of that should matter to Sue," stated Lucy firmly. "We all know she doesn't care about money and things like that, or she wouldn't live in a little house on the beach and make her own dresses from raggy sheets. That's what's so wonderful about her. She won't mind if people in the factory get the money--in fact she'll probably think it's a good idea."

"I'm sure she doesn't care about the money," continued Dad, "but in a funny way she will care about her father, even when she disagrees with him. I believe she loves him. She hates to see him unhappy, becoming a sad old man just because she doesn't do what he wants."

"But he has no right to make her do what he wants."

"Perhaps not, but she still feels it's her fault if he's angry or lonely or upset. It's called 'feeling guilty'. You know what people are like."

"So does this mean he's going to object to Sue getting engaged?" asked Lucy angrily. "Have we got to allow him to ruin everything just because he doesn't like the idea of his daughter being happy with new people?"

"We don't know that yet," answered Dad honestly. "We don't know how he's going to react when he hears about us, but we have to face the possibility that when Sue tells him she's going to marry me he might explode in a fit of rage."

"If he explodes we'll be rid of him," said Sam slyly.

"But you're not going to let this happen, are you?" Now Lucy was almost crying. "You can't let him take her away. You're engaged!"

"Quiet, my girl." Dad's voice was kindly but firm. "Do you really think anyone could take Sue away from what she wants to do?

She's gone to talk to him, tell him about us, and explain what has to happen. He may not like it but he'll have to accept it. Sue's a free woman."

"Yes, but he'll still have some wicked millionaire's trick to destroy all our lives. We must do something!"

"Now calm down, Lucy. Let's just wait and see what happens after Sue and her father have had their talk. She's probably going to have dinner with him and stay aboard the yacht overnight. We'll see her tomorrow."

"I wish I could believe that," said Lucy with glum anger.

"We may never see her again," said Sam.

"Yes we will. I had to let her go to the yacht: I'm marrying her, not making her a prisoner. What we really have to do is make friends with her father and let him see we're sensible people who can give his daughter a good life. We mustn't seem awkward or difficult. You understand that, don't you?"

"I understand her father's big trouble. I don't like him, and we'll show him how much we love Sue!"

At last they went to their bedrooms, but none felt like sleeping. Lucy and Sam could hear Dad moving around and imagined him looking through the window with the binoculars all night. Restless themselves, they climbed out of their beds and crept to the window, hoping for a glimpse of life aboard *Lady Susannah*. At least the yacht remained at anchor with her lights still twinkling. They imagined Sue having a late and unhappy dinner with her stern father, perhaps in some richly-panelled saloon where she would be expected to wear an ordinary dress and shoes; where her engagement ring of Dad's own hair, her mermaid's necklace, her goddess's crown, and her beautiful love for her new family would all be scorned or laughed at or dismissed as ridiculous. She might be snatched away by this angry man. Even worse, she might leave of her own accord if he somehow convinced her that she would be pleasing him and be happier herself in a more conventional life. In the dead of night, all dangers and horrors and wild imaginings began to seem real to Lucy and she told herself to stay calm. It was very unlikely that the yacht would slip her moorings with Sue as unwilling captive. If that did happen, Lucy reckoned Sue would jump into the sea and escape anyway, making a rapid swim back to her island and a loving reunion in this cosy house. No, more likely there would be some kind of meeting, a conference, a grown-up's talk-- which Lucy knew would be the most dangerous and threatening development of all. She decided that would be when she and Sam would act--and she began to plot a scheme in her mind, a scheme that slowly turned her anxious tears into mischievous smiles.

Chapter 17   Council of War, Plan for Love

Eventually, sleep overtook each of them, and there were a few hours of oblivion in the house--but Lucy woke very early and climbed stealthily out of her bed. In different circumstances she would have stood rapt at the door, drinking in the cool air, wondering at the purity of pink and grey clouds in the luminous sky, alive to every sensation. As it was, she looked quickly to check that the yacht was still at her moorings. She was, with no movement on board. Listening at Dad's door and hearing no sound of his being awake, Lucy crept back to Sam's bunk. She realised thankfully that she would not need to wake him, as he stirred into consciousness at her approach.

"Shhh," Lucy whispered in his ear. "Nothing's wrong. I was coming to wake you anyway. We must talk before Dad gets up. I have a plan."

"A plan?" Sam was properly awake now, swinging his legs over the edge of his bed.

"Yes, a plan to make sure that Sue marries Dad with no trouble from her father....."

"Brilliant!" Sam put on his shirt and trousers.

".....but we can't talk about it in here. We mustn't wake Dad or let him think there's anything peculiar going on. Come outside very quietly and I'll tell you the whole idea."

They stepped silently through the rooom on bare feet. Opening the front door was an agonising business of ensuring it didn't creak or rattle--and this took long, nerve-racking moments. Then they were outside in the fresh dawn, closing the door gently again and feeling completely awake in the wide splendours of sea and sky, their feet chilly in the dew-covered grass.

"Should've worn shoes," grumbled Sam. "Dunno how Sue manages."

They walked silently round the house and sat down on one of the planks of driftwood which had been securing the motorcycle cover since the storm. The first peep of sun came to warm them.

"We're all right here," said Lucy softly, "as long as we talk quietly. Now, it all depends on a meeting with Dad, Sue, and her father. There's bound to be one: you know how grown-ups always have to talk things over instead of just doing them. Well, we have to make sure the meeting is held in one of the houses here, *not* on the yacht. So, here's what we do....."

Sam grew more and more excited as Lucy explained her plan. More than once she had to tell him to stay calm and quiet, not wake Dad, and to make sure that when Dad did wake up his suspicion wasn't aroused. Sam knew Lucy was right and did his best to contain the thrills that kept running through him. This morning there was a plan; but soon there would be a full-blooded adventure to make exploring, rowing, map-making, bird-watching, and even swimming with a mermaid seem tame!

".....okay, Sam?" Lucy concluded twenty minutes later. "Not a word to Dad. We'd better go back now and make him breakfast: we've got to keep his strength up."

"And ours," added Sam, already tired and hungry after his vivid imagination of what was to come.

The sun climbed up the sky and Dad climbed out of bed. He seemed delighted that Lucy and Sam were already up and had made breakfast. While they ate, they discussed what might happen during the day.

"Sue should come back off the yacht this morning," suggested Dad. "She obviously had dinner with her father and a long talk. I'd like to know what she's said about us and how the old boy has taken the idea of her getting married. Anyway, we'll find out soon enough. There'll have to be some sort of meeting."

"A meeting, yes," Lucy replied as innocently as she could. "Sam and I have been thinking about that. We thought it would be a good idea to have the meeting here. We would look very friendly and polite inviting Sue's father here. He could see how we live and what nice people we are and that there's really nothing to worry about when Sue does marry you and joins our family."

"Mmm," Dad agreed, "very thoughtful and sensible of you."

"Then we'd be on our home ground," added Sam, "and not have to go aboard the yacht where we could be kidnapped and locked in the hold. Always better to stay out of the enemy camp."

Lucy gave him a furious look.

"Sue's father is *not* an enemy, Sam."

"I thought he was," said Sam with disappointment.

"Yes," Dad was musing, "a very good idea. I hope Sue comes back soon and we can have a proper talk about this. My real fear is that she's been upset or bullied by her father; he might have put subtle, unfair pressure on her. I hate to think of that happening."

"We'll fix him," growled Sam.

"Just get busy with that," snapped Lucy, handing Sam the washing-up liquid, "and be quiet."

The morning wore on. There was no sign of life aboard *Lady Susannah*. At length Lucy said:

"We could row over in *Albatross* and offer to bring them ashore."

"Maybe later," said Dad.

"We won't need to," said Sam suddenly. "Look--she's on her way."

They saw Sue emerge on to the yacht's deck, her swimsuit now its usual rich purple in the sunlight. A moment later she had dived into the sea and was swimming easily towards the shore.

"Here she comes!" cried Sam excitedly, Lucy and Dad following him down the beach.

Dad had brought a towel. As Sue walked from the quiet waves, looking as tall and golden and beautiful as ever, he wrapped it around her. The magic of seeing her for the first time was renewed, along with feelings of huge relief that she was actually among them once more. Dad kissed her and helped her dry her hair. Lucy and Sam kissed her and received sea-wet kisss in return, but her smile was only a faint one, and the children feared the worst.

"As usual he's come to take me home at the end of the holidays," her voice was quite flat and matter-of-fact, "and as usual I won't go. But this year he's got something else to think about. I told him everything about us."

"We knew you would," said Lucy.

"You had to," said Sam.

"And?" asked Dad, holding her hands.

"He's dead against it of course." She took her hands away to squeeze the towel around her body, chilled with the morning air. "He disapproves automatically of any potential husband he hasn't chosen for me himself. Not that I care--and he knows I don't care. All the same, his final comment was that he doesn't know you."

"He will," said Dad with firm resolve.

"We'd like him to come here and meet us," Lucy plunged in with her offer. "He can get to know Dad, see us all together, and realise how happy you are with us."

"Yes," now Sue smiled more happily, "that's a great idea. He deserves to meet you, but he also needs to. It'll do him more good than he can guess."

"Breakfast," ordered Dad, still rubbing her dry.

"Hot coffee, please," requested Sue. "I missed you," she confessed sweetly, "I missed you all like crazy. My father will just have to accept I've found someone I love."

"We've found someone, too," said Lucy, taking Sue's hand as they went up the beach.

"All of us," added Sam, taking her other hand.

Chapter 18   *Albatross* to the Rescue

An atmosphere of unease continued to fill the morning as Lucy and Sam waited for an opportunity to put their secret plan into action. Their hearts sank when Sue announced she would swim out to the yacht again and invite her father ashore for lunch. That would achieve only part of the scheme; if father and daughter rowed back to the beach in the yacht's inflatable dinghy, Lucy and Sam would have to think of something else to complete their plan. Dad also looked worried when Sue disappeared into the sea again. Lucy imagined how he must be feeling at each loss of the woman he had only just found.....but everyone felt better when at last they saw Sue run back into the dunes to be dried once more by Dad.

"He's agreed to join us for lunch," Sue explained between gasps of air. "There's a much colder current today," she added, thankful for Dad's fluffy towel and his warm hugs. "I'll try to stay out of the water now."

They went into the house. Sue returned from the bathroom wearing their biggest towel.

"It's a pink sarong!" exclaimed Lucy.

"You don't mind if I rinse out my costume in your sink? I'll get some dry clothes from my place later."

"There's nothing special for this lunch," warned Dad. "More bacon and eggs."

"He's jolly lucky to get that," replied Sue, undaunted, "and he'd better like it. It's you he's coming to meet, not the inside of your larder."

"Is he fat enough already?" ventured Sam.

"Don't be cheeky, Sam." Lucy produced another hot coffee and handed it to Sue. "You and Dad stay together here. Sam and I will row across in *Albatross* and offer your father a lift back to shore. That way he needn't bother to launch his own boat--and he should like the idea of children coming to see him. Isn't it true that deep down, all angry old men really love children? You'll see. We'll be polite and we'll make him very welcome. He shouldn't object to that; he'll understand it's all for the best."

Sam had put his hands in his pockets and was biting his lip to stop himself squirming with excitement at Lucy's crafty proposal. If the grown-ups accepted this, the plan was on! There was a moment of silence, then he and the others saw Sue smile properly for the first time that morning.

"See what a family I'm marrying into? Who could possibly object to such adorable children?"

"It's the adorable father he's got to like," added Dad with a jokey but anxious grin.

"Oh, you're a separate problem." Sue gave him a playful pat on the head. "We'll sort you out later."

"Is this really a good idea," Dad looked out of the window, "sending them over by themselves?"

"Yes. Why not? I've told him about your delightful children. Now he can meet them on their own terms and see how sensible, considerate, and resourceful they are."

"Mmm," Dad didn't sound convinced. "Two kids handling that little boat, strong current, choppy water, getting a big man off a yacht, over the side and down into a skittery little thing....."

"Shouldn't be a problem. She had four aboard last time," Sue reminded him of their voyage in *Albatross* with the poet, "and there are easy steps off the stern of the yacht. Just remember, when you help him into the boat," she turned to Lucy and Sam, "my father doesn't swim."

"We'll certainly remember that," said Sam, cheerily.

* * *

"Right!" Lucy took Sam into the bedroom while Dad was preparing the table for lunch. "This is it. We're very lucky it's worked out this way."

She was wearing tight shorts and a close-fitting top and had tied her hair back with an especially severe ribbon.

"Are you properly dressed under that lot?" She pointed at Sam's shirt and shorts.

"Oh yes," he smiled.

"Remember, no shoes for this job."

Sam took his off.

"Okay, Dad," they came out of the bedroom. "We're off now."

"Stripped down for some serious rowing, I see," said Sue.

"Are you sure you can manage that boat?" asked Dad.

"Of course they can," smiled Sue. "The sea's calm enough today."

"'Bye!"

Lucy and Sam hurried out of the house, a huge giggle exploding between them, but they became serious again as they trotted down the beach and dragged *Albatross* from her secret place in the dunes. Fitting the rowlocks and the oars, they soon had her afloat and were splashing aboard, Lucy at the oars, Sam in the stern.

Sue had been right. Once the boat had been pushed through the small breakers they found the sea was very calm. Soon they were into smooth water with none of the swell they had experienced on their last memorable row in *Albatross*. Down here on the sea the houses in the dunes looked far away. They turned and waved to Dad and Sue, who waved back.

"I wish they weren't watching us all the time," said Sam.

"Don't worry," Lucy swung *Albatross* out to sea. "It's all working out perfectly."

Lucy rowed with strength and ease, her legs drying in the sunshine. Sam thought her bare arms were showing the muscles of a real sailor-girl, but she was a little starboard-side-heavy, and he had to keep correcting her course for *Lady Susannah*. Soon the great yacht was looming ahead of them. From sea-level she looked massive; heavier and broader than they had first thought, gleaming white, flashing with brass and varnish, towering into the sky with her masts and wires.

"Row round her first for a good look," said Sam.

Lucy began to circumnavigate the yacht. Rich-looking curtains could be seen behind the windows of her saloon, her tiny port-holes and spacious wheelhouse looked equally fascinating, her perfectly-proportioned prow and bowsprit made her an awesome sight head-on, and the varnished teak steps, gently swilled and sucked by the sea, were a mysteriously inviting feature of her stern.

"Always something rather spooky about rowing close to a big ship," remarked Lucy.

"She's not *that* big," observed Sam. "Look," he read the lettering on her stern, "*Lady Susannah*, *Cannes*. That's in the South of France, where rich people live."

"I didn't think he'd sailed all that way," grumbled Lucy.

"That's just the port of registry," stated Sam. "It doesn't mean Sue's father has come from there."

"I know that," answered Lucy. "He probably has, though, if he's a multi-multi-millionaire."

"*Lady Susannah*. D'you think the yacht really is named after Sue?"

"Could be."

"The English name doesn't really go with the French name, does it?"

"He's so rich it doesn't matter."

"Shall I hail him, then?"

"Yes, go ahead," answered Lucy. She stood *Albatross* more than a good rope's throw off the yacht's port side and rested her oars.

"Ahoy there!" shouted Sam. No sign of life appeared on the yacht. He looked at Lucy and Lucy nodded at him and he called again. "Ahoy there *Lady Susannah*! *Albatross* alongside and ready to go ashore!"

There was only the faint cloop and ripple of the sea round the big white hull and the gentle slap of water under the empty stern steps.....then she rocked a little as a large figure appeared in her after well.

"What the Devil's all this shouting about?"

The figure seemed to be all bald head and golden beard, then it heaved itself on deck and Sue's father was revealed in his white clothes, glowering at them from the stern rail.

"Well?" he boomed.

"Good morning, sir!" Lucy pulled on her oars and swung *Albatross* neatly under the yacht's stern. "We're your new grandchildren--or we're very shortly going to be. We've come to row you ashore for lunch."

"Ah yes," the golden beard wagged down at them, "I've heard about you two--and a cheeky pair of pups you look."

"We thought we'd save you the trouble of launching your own boat," Lucy continued as charmingly as she could. "You go in the bow, Sam," she ordered quietly, then called up again. "I'll bring her in astern to your steps, sir, and give you a hand down." She stood up with a smile. "We wouldn't want our new grandad to get wet feet on our first day together."

"New grandad indeed," he snorted. "You presumptious young rascals. I haven't been sucked into your wretched family yet, and don't you forget it."

"You'll like our father, sir," Lucy continued as if oblivious to the insults. "He's an ex-Navy man. He's very impressed that you sail your big yacht single-handed. He'll admire her when he comes aboard."

"Will he indeed? I want a good look at him first. All right," he came to the top of the steps, "let's get it over with."

"Steady as you go, sir." Lucy extended a slender arm and felt her hand grasped in a big hot paw as the heavy man's deck shoes squeaked down the steps and he settled himself uneasily in the stern of *Albatross*. The bow rode up alarmingly and Sam lay out as far as he could to counterbalance the weight. "There." Lucy fitted her toes carefully between the large shoes now filling much of the space on *Albatross's* sandy boards. "Comfy?" She gave Sue's father a glittering smile, put her knees together, took up the oars, and pulled gently away from the yacht.

"Comfy indeed. Ha! This little tub'll go under if anyone hiccups, then you'll drown us all."

"*Albatross* is a good boat," said Lucy calmly. "You could row to Norway in her--if you were fit enough."

"Ha! And how old are you?"

"I'm fourteen," answered Lucy, "and my brother Sam is eleven. This is our best holiday ever--and it'll be yours, too. It's already turned out to be Sue's best holiday."

"Holiday? What she needs is a good dose of responsibility."

"She'll get it, looking after us," smiled Lucy. "We are a whole new career for her."

"Career? Pah! She couldn't hold down a tuppenny-ha'penny job!"

"She could be a brilliant swimming teacher," put in Sam.

"Hmm." The big man looked them up and down. "Trust my daughter to take up with an impertinent pair of raggedy, barefoot brats."

Lucy had pulled *Albatross* well away from the yacht. Now she pointed her bow at the horizon, rested her oars, and looked directly at Sue's father.

"You *should* trust your daughter, sir. She's a remarkable woman, very clever and independent and honest and loving. You should be proud of her, not make her life a misery."

"How dare you?" cried Sue's father. He was twitching with rage but obviously unwilling to wave his arms about from his unsteady perch on the small stern seat. He wagged his beard and stared with fury instead. "How dare you lecture me about my own daughter and things you know nothing about?"

"Because we do know your daughter, and we love her. She loves us, too. She especially loves our father, who loves her madly, though he's sometimes too shy to show it. And you can be sure he's going to treat her better than you have. That's why you have to give your blessing to their engagement--and be pleased when they marry."

"This is too much!" Now in a towering rage, Sue's father was turning purple with beads of sweat breaking out on his bald head. "I insist you take me back to the yacht! You can stick your blasted lunch where you like and bring your blasted father out here some other time-- but not before you've learned some manners!"

Lucy gripped the oars.

"It's you who needs to learn some manners, sir. You know your daughter loves my father; she must have told you the truth last night, if you were decent enough to listen to it. Now, do you or do you not give your blessing?"

"I most certainly do not!"

"Will you come to lunch and meet my father now, or will you wait for a wedding invitation?"

"Blast you, girl! Get me back to my yacht!"

"Right," Lucy lifted the oars. "Over you go, Sam."

"What?" spluttered Sue's father, seeing Sam slide out of his loose shirt.

"Hurry up, Sam. You know what we agreed."

"Yes, yes, okay--aaaghh!" The boat rocked dangerously as Sam tumbled over the bow. "It's colder than ever!" he shouted. "It's freezing!"

"Have an oar."

Lucy unshipped one and dropped it into the sea for Sam to grasp. Then she dropped the other one over the other side and followed it into the water as neatly as she could, holding on to the gunwale as *Albatross* lurched sternwards under Sue's father's weight. Sensing the danger, he flung himself forward and thumped on to Lucy's vacated seat amidships. Now there were no oars to hold on to, he gripped the gunwales in a mixture of terror and fury. All this had happened in a few moments. Lucy and Sam were in the water, swimming lazily with the oars like shipwrecked survivors clinging to flotsam, *Albatross* was drifting oarless in the bay, and Sue's father was alone on the North Sea.

"Blast you! Come back here! What the Devil d'you think you're doing? Are you mad?"

"You're right, Sam," Lucy commented languidly from her oar. "The water's jolly cold for this time of year. I'd say it could kill an old unfit man in, what, half an hour?"

"Come back at once, d'you hear?"

"You'll be swept out to Norway," said Sam. "You'll be stung by jellyfish and eaten by crabs."

"Come back at once!" Panic now entered the voice alongside fury. "I can't swim!"

Lucy ducked her head under and came up smiling.

"You really can't swim?"

"Certainly not!" came the bellowed reply. "What d'you think ships are for? And swimming's a filthy business: water full of germs and toilet paper."

"Perhaps where you live," answered Lucy, "but it's wonderfully clean and cold up here. You should have let your daughter teach you."

"I never let my daughter do ridiculous things if I can possibly help it."

"No. She does them by herself--and a good thing for her, I say."

"You cheeky brats. I'll have you locked up for this."

"You'll have to get out of that boat first." Sam swam up to the bow of *Albatross* and gave her a shove. "Norway's that way."

"I demand an end to this!"

"The end is in your own hands," said Lucy calmly, resting both gleaming arms along her oar. "By the way, d'you think I have pretty shoulders? I'm not as grown up as Sue yet, and nowhere near as beautiful, but there's a boy at school who thinks I have pretty shoulders, especially when I'm swimming. D'you think I would suit my hair really short like Sue's?"

"Shut up, you hussy, and get me out of this boat!"

Lucy and Sam were delighted to observe that *Albatross* really was drifting away from the yacht on a gently Northward current. They began to wonder if they had been seen from the shore. This whole escapade would be ruined if Sue suddenly swam out to rescue her father, but there was no sign of anyone outside the house, and it was quite easy to keep paddling softly in the water, using their oars as floats.

"Do you hear me?" shouted Sue's father. "You've played your stupid game, now get me back to my yacht!"

"You know what you have to do," called Lucy over the increasing distance, "and you have to mean it, and not go back on your word."

The mildest swell appeared, lifting them all gently towards the open sea. Lucy and Sam kicked towards the shore. Long moments passed in the silent bay. A Fulmar swept across the empty water, the blue horizon stretched away.

"All right," growled Sue's father. "All right, blast you! Your father has my blessing, my daughter can marry him, she can be your new mother if she's crazy enough to want to be, you can all inherit my millions. See if I care who gets the blasted money. She'll be so rich she can live in a shack with you lot for the rest of her life and never buy a decent dress or wear shoes. See if I care. Now let me out of this blasted boat!"

The silence of the bay continued, broken only by gently rippling water as Lucy and Sam steered themselves round to face Sue's father over an increasing width of cold sea.

"Promise?" called Lucy.

"Yes, yes, blast you!"

"Without using swear words?" added Sam.

"Yes.....all right.....yes!"

"And you'll come to lunch and meet our father and respect him and try to understand your daughter?" Lucy flashed another smile across the water.

"Yes." Sue's father suddenly folded his arms over his massive chest while a whole new expression came to his face.

"An excellent decision, sir," Lucy beamed at him and swam closer to *Albatross*. "If you promise truly to respect your daughter and my father and treat them as sensible grown-ups, we'll row you ashore now--or we can swim back with the good news and let you drift for a while. It'll calm you down. Lunch isn't good on an angry stomach."

The new expression on the big face turned into a golden-bearded smile.

"Respect, eh? Is that what you want? Well, you'll get it." Sue's father began to chuckle: something Lucy and Sam had not expected, and they trod water at their floating oars in some surprise as they watched amusement begin to shake his large body. "Honestly, anyone who has brought up two youngsters to be as resourceful as you deserves respect--and he's obviously had his hands full. But I'll have to tell him you clever monkeys are a piece of cake compared to my daughter." At this, he began to laugh openly and put his hands back on the gunwales of *Albatross*. "She'll have him for breakfast. No-one's ever been able to deal with her. Ha, ha--she'll lick you all into shape. She'll inherit my millions but she'll keep you all in rags in that beach-hut! A-ha.....a-ha-ha-ha.....a-ha-ha-ha-ha-ha-ha-ha.....!" He flung an arm up to indicate the distant house--and fell backwards out of *Albatross*.

The huge splash shocked Lucy and Sam into action. They thrust forward with their oars; at the same time *Albatross* rode a newly-crested wave. Behind it they saw large legs and feet sticking out of the water--then watched them slowly sink.

"Come on!" shouted Sam. "He's right under!"

The sea erupted in front of them. Up came the huge and bearded face, blowing and snorting like an enraged walrus.

"Blast!" it yelled--and went under again.

"Get the oars under his arms!" cried Lucy.

The head surfaced again, streaming water. The staring eyes focussed on the children and the huge arms thrashed the water in wild panic.

"The oars!" cried Lucy again, pushing hers forward.

"Here's the other one!" Sam powered his oar through the water as Sue's father sank again.

"This time," ordered Lucy. "We've got to get him this time or he won't come up alive. Ready?"

The head came up once more, right in front of them. They each grabbed a shoulder and pushed their oars under the arms.

"Grab on to these," said Sam. "You'll be all right."

A spout of water burst from the bearded mouth. The blue eyes opened again; the mouth sucked in air.

"Help," came the whimper, followed by a cough and a lot more water.

"Oh, control yourself, will you?" said Lucy sharply. "Just hang on to these."

While Lucy swam to grab *Albatross*, Sam had turned to face the shore and was pointing at figures running down the beach.

"Oh no," he cried, "we've been seen!"

Sue and Dad had entered the water and were swimming out to meet them.

"We'll be in real trouble now," said Sam.

"We'll worry about that later." Lucy had hold of *Albatross*, but realised it would be quite impossible to get Sue's father aboard. "Steer him back to the yacht," she told Sam. "He can go up the steps."

Sam held the ends of the oars and did breast-stroke with his legs.

"You look like a frog pushing an iceberg," laughed Lucy.

As they had expected, Sue was first to arrive at the scene. Her powerful crawl ploughed to a stop and her shining face came up.

"Well, Father," she snapped. "What a ridiculous spectacle! I've never been more ashamed of you. It's obvious I can't let you out of my sight for ten minutes."

A second submarine surfaced nearby. It was Dad.

"What the.....?"

"Don't say it," Sue stopped him, "and don't blame the children. If I were you I'd thank them. We were watching you through binoculars. We saw the whole thing."

"Are you all right?" asked Dad breathlessly: amazed, concerned, and exhilarated all at the same time.

"Perfectly," said Lucy, looking comfortable in the water alongside Sam at *Albatross*'s gunwale.

"Well, you can give me your explanation when we get back-- and it had better be a good one."

"And you, Father," Sue turned with chilly elegance to the bloated figure, still gasping between the oars like a polar bear stuck on a waterlogged railway line. "Are you alive? Are you able to speak? Can you say anything pleasant or worthwhile?"

"Blast!"

The big man thumped the water with his fists, slid off the oars, went under, and came up again to face hoots of laughter led by Sue's white teeth flashing in the sunlight.

Chapter 19   The Poet's Farewell

By the end of the day everyone was ashore, everyone was dry, and everyone had done as much arm-waving and voice-raising as had been necessary to get these things out of their systems. Dad gave Lucy and Sam a telling-off--but it wasn't a very good telling-off, because he kept interrupting it with grins and chuckles as he recalled the outrageously inventive brilliance of his children's plan and replayed its hilarious outcome in his mind. Instead of provoking a family argument, Lucy and Sam's escapade had produced a family story which was obviously going to be told over and over as the years went by--and probably exaggerated beyond its true events--but the children knew how narrow a line they had walked between the serious trouble they had just avoided and the happy result which seemed to be working out.

The much-planned lunch was abandoned in favour of dinner aboard *Lady Susannah*, where Sue's father made a long speech. Nobody expected him to thank Lucy and Sam for teaching him a lesson in love, but that is exactly what he did. He even admitted he had been wrong in not trusting his daughter. Then he gave his blessing to her marriage to Dad, and promised he would pay for the wedding whenever and wherever she wanted it.

"You wont need to buy a wedding dress," Sam interrupted. "She's already made a beautiful one."

"That was an engagement-party dress," said Lucy quietly. "She'll need another one for the wedding."

"I'll make that as well," grinned Sue. "Anyone got a spare white sheet?"

"I'll buy you a satin sheet," said Lucy.

It was agreed that at the end of the holiday Sue would sail to London with her father, while Dad would travel home with Lucy and Sam in the motorcycle and sidecar; then they would all meet again for the wedding.

"Don't worry," Sue whispered to Lucy, "the *real* wedding will be back here."

"On the island?" begged Lucy.

"At our cairn with your shell in it?" pleaded Sam.

"Yes," she smiled. "You can be Bridesmaid and Best Man all over again."

"And Dad can give you another ring," said Sam.

"Just us," said Lucy thoughtfully, "with the sea stretching away, and only the sky above us. That'll be the best wedding ever."

* * *

The next few days were filled with plans and talk and the surprising discovery that Sue's father--who had at first seemed such a monster--could now be a friendly and genial host. He arranged a short cruise aboard *Lady Susannah*. Lucy and Sam were amazed at the yacht's luxury, but more intrigued by the seals they saw swimming South from the Farne Islands, surfacing around the yacht's hull, looking at them with their appealing puppy-dog faces, blinking their lustrous eyes, and opening and closing their nostrils.

"I wish we could do that," observed Sam. "I mean for going under water. They swim brilliantly."

"Sue's almost as good," said Lucy.

Then came another expedition to the castle, and Dad was preparing the motorcycle for its long ride South. Anxiety began to take over from excitement as their separation from Sue drew closer.

"Don't worry, Dad," Lucy tried to re-assure him. "She's not going to be snatched away by her wicked father. He's not really so wicked after all, is he? He's been quite nice. He just had to get to know us all."

"Yes," Dad grumbled, "but I still don't trust him completely. I don't like his idea of making the voyage down to London a 'cooling off period'. People who are in love shouldn't have to 'cool off'. I'm surprised Sue agreed to it."

"Well, it's just a yacht-cruise down the coast," Lucy did her best to cheer him up. "She'll keep her father company for a few days, that's all. Anyway, Dad," she smiled, "you're not supposed to be together until the wedding. You'll just have to put up with doing things properly."

The preparations continued, and a feeling of desolation came into the cosy little house as Dad packed more of their kit around the motorcycle and sidecar. When Harry Baxter re-appeared one day, Sam rushed through the dunes with the news, then led him back to Skylark Cottage.

"It's the poet!" cried Sam. "I've told him everything."

"Well," there were smiles and handshakes, "congratulations. This is quite something."

"It needs a poem," demanded Sam.

"Oh," chuckled the poet dismissively, "there are more than enough words at weddings as it is. When are you going back to London--and how are you all going to fit in and on that motorbike arrangement?"

He was told of the separate travel plans.

"I'll come and see you off," he promised.

* * *

The day of their departure dawned as clear and blue as the others which had brought them such delight in Albatross Bay. Sam had wanted cloud and rain to mark the melancholy end of their holiday; then he realised there was no real sorrow, rather a sense of excitement at the new adventurous life Sue would surely bring into the family.

There had been no great farewell to Sue: deliberately so, because no-one really wanted to admit there was going to be a long separation while they travelled to London and no-one wanted to make a sad scene of parting. They all preferred to think about meeting again for the wedding, which was to take place as soon as possible. So, very early that morning, there had been warm but brief hugs and kisses on the beach below the houses, and only a few tears--then Sue and her father had rowed out to *Lady Susannah* in the yacht's inflatable boat.

"She should really be swimming out," Sam had remarked.

"I'd rather swim back to you than away from you," Sue had replied.

With Sue aboard the yacht it now seemed right to say farewell to their special place as well as to their special person.

"It's not really goodbye," said Lucy as they went along the beach, "more *au revoir*, as the French say."

"Of course. We'll be back for the wedding," said Sam as they climbed the North Lookout Dune, "the *real* wedding, that is, on the island."

There it lay, ringed with dark blue sea, just as it was drawn on Sam and Lucy's map. They could see their cairn, the little boats in the anchorage, and the much larger *Lady Susannah*--already having her diesel engine run up, producing puffs of grey smoke.

"Look," Lucy pointed to a new flag in the yacht's rigging. "She's flying the Blue Peter."

"Sailing day," said Sam.

The great curving beach swept from North to South beneath them and led their gaze to the distant castle on its cliff. High up here, on the pointed summit of the dune, they felt again the freshness and purity of the air.

"Albatross Bay," breathed Sam, almost to himself. "A wonderful place."

Another engine crackled into life, a little to the North and behind them.

"Dad's testing the bike," said Lucy. "Let's go back."

On their return to the cottage, they found the poet admiring the chrome fittings on the motorbike and helping Dad load the sidecar with bags and boxes.

"Come on, you two," he said, "your Dad needs all the help he can get. I never knew you could pack so much on to a motorbike. Where's the bride-to-be in all this?"

"She's on the yacht," explained Dad, "talking to her father."

"Talk, talk, talk," grinned the poet. "It's what I've always said: too many words at weddings. So," he fished into the depths of a pocket, "here's the antidote." He presented two identical envelopes and gave one to Dad. "Open it on the way to the wedding," he smiled mysteriously. "And this one," he turned to Lucy and Sam, showing them the other envelope, "I'll have to hurry up and deliver this to Sue before she sails."

"In *Albatross*?" asked Sam.

"Of course. You wouldn't catch *me* swimming that distance, even if I could keep the paper dry. I know there's been enough dangerous watersport out there recently."

"We'd come with you," began Lucy, "if we hadn't already said our goodbyes.....you know.....we'd have to say them all again....."

"I understand perfectly, and you've got plenty to do here. I'd better hurry."

"But what is it?" asked Sam. "What's in the envelope?"

"It's a couplet."

"What's a couplet?"

"Two lines of poetry, of course," Lucy told him.

"Two lines of *rhyming* poetry, to be absolutely accurate," added the poet.

"Just two lines?" Sam sounded disappointed.

"They're the best two lines I've ever written, if I say so myself" smiled the poet, "and I do. Now--travel safely. I'll give you a wave as you go off."

With that, he disappeared into the dunes.

"He's an odd fellow, isn't he?" said Dad quietly. "Come along then, there's still loads of packing to do."

Chapter 20   The Mermaid's Kiss

A light Westerly breeze had sprung up, fluttering the Blue Peter in *Lady Susannah*'s rigging, and it was now clear that the yacht would be able to make her departure under sail. Sue and her father could be seen on deck, he in his gleaming whites, she in blue jeans and a loose red shirt. They were untying some ropes and hauling on others, and the first sail appeared: a small jib hoisted at her bow.

"Where shall we wave from?" asked Dad

"The North Lookout Dune, of course," decided Sam.

They climbed the sandy track to the top, taking the binoculars and their mixed feelings once more up into the fresh blue air.

Lady Susannah's engine growled as her anchor was raised and she was turned to stand Southwards under bare poles. Then the engine was cut and billows of canvas appeared as vast white sails were hoisted on her mainmast and mizzen.

"They're off!" cried Sam, waving furiously. "Wave your hanky, Lucy!"

A nearby crackle of paper disturbed the children.

"But Dad," they objected, "you're not supposed to open the envelope until you're on the way to the wedding!"

"We *are* on our way," said Dad, looking down at a piece of blue paper. All eyes were distracted from the wide spectacle of the yacht creeping Southwards down the vast bay to a concentration upon tiny handwritten words. A slow smile spread over Dad's face, then he looked longingly out to sea again.

"But what is it? What is it? What does it say?"

Dad held out the paper with his silent smile. The children took it and read:

> *When words won't do, remember this:*
> *We say it better with a kiss.*

"He's right, isn't he?" grinned Lucy. "What a great piece of poetry!"

Their thoughts were interrupted by a distant shout. It was a loud, strong, man's voice, obviously coming from *Lady Susannah*. They looked up and passed the binoculars around. The big yacht continued to slide across the bay, but with a new commotion at her stern. Sue's father shouted again. They couldn't make out the words, but saw he was waving a red shirt in one hand and a blue paper in the other. Then many things seemed to happen at once. A suntanned body dived into the sea, the distant splash coming to their ears moments later, and a close spatter of sand hit the children's legs as Dad set off at a run down the dune.

"No," Lucy held Sam's arm as he was about to follow. "Don't do anything, don't say anything."

They took turns with the binoculars, watching Dad sprint across the beach and pull off his shirt. They watched Sue's golden head dipping and surfacing as her powerful crawl brought her inshore. They watched Dad run into the sea. Before very long they saw the two heads together in the bright water: one dark, one golden. They watched a long and passionate kiss.

Another shout distracted them again, this time from the dunes.

"Hooray!"

They swung the binoculars on to the land.

"Hooray!"

It was the poet, cheering from outside his house.

"Hooray!"

They returned their attention to the heads bobbing darkly in the glittering sea between the white sails of *Lady Susannah* and the white line of waves on the beach.

"She's read the poem, too, hasn't she?" said Sam.

"Of course," said Lucy.

They watched the heads being lifted and lowered by the gentle swell, and again came that peculiar sense of music born of sea-light and sun-sparkle, cold air and vast water, a wild song of open oceans that was also a cosy melody of home.

"What *are* they saying to each other?" asked Sam, peering intently through the binoculars at the two heads face-to-face in the sea.

"Nothing," said Lucy, reading the words again. "This is my favourite poem ever!"

THE END

Printed in the United Kingdom by
Lightning Source UK Ltd., Milton Keynes
141893UK00002B/20/P